HAVE YOU GOT A MINUTE?

The Rookie HR Years

E Harvey & J Field

Fisher King Publishing

Have you got a minute?

ISBN 978-1-913170-82-0

Published by
Fisher King Publishing
The Studio
Arthington Lane
Pool in Wharfedale
LS21 1JZ
England

www.fisherkingpublishing.co.uk

Cover design by Claire Marsden at Studio 37

For Matt, Will, Maddie, Al, Leo,
Orlaith, Sundays and Thursdays
without whom this book would
never have happened.

PROLOGUE

Name: Gemma Walters
Age: 23
Time and Place: Our story begins in November 1997. To set the scene, Britpop is King, but Robbie and the Spice Girls dominate the pop charts. 24/7 television is firmly in place and Channel 5 has just been launched on terrestrial TV. This is the year that the world lost Princess Diana, Mother Teresa, Notorious B.I.G. Some even mourned the passing of Cheryl Stark from Neighbours. On the bright side, we gained Dolly the cloned sheep and a glimpse into life on Mars through the American spacecraft, Pathfinder. Hong Kong has been handed back to China (like it was ours to take in the first place!) and the Labour Party has been returned to government by the British people in a landslide general election victory. The film Titanic has been released and will go on to become one of the biggest grossing films of all time. Over the pond, the Bill Clinton and Monica Lewinski affair is in full swing. Luckily for us, *that* stain on *that* dress has not yet come to light.

Imagine that you've been transported back to another world in the Tardis (although the Doctor himself was taking a well-earned rest in a galaxy far, far, away at this point). It's a world that you might well find unrecognisable. Firstly, it is not the politically correct health and safety obsessed environment that we find ourselves in now. There were rules and regulations, but employers, employees and their union representatives did not hold back when it came to strong opinions; they would fly around the workplace like little rubber pellets, easily catching those in the firing line completely off guard. The world of HR during this time and place was a tricky road to navigate; the learning curve was steep, but there was never a dull moment.

This is a book made up of a veritable feast of experiences taken from the rich tapestry of my first years in Human Resources or HR for short, albeit a work of fiction. I feel lucky to have worked in the field of HR for over twenty years. I've worked with some incredible people - from 'salt of the earth' northern folk to CEOs in corporate America. I can honestly say that people are generally brilliant - whichever walk of life they're from. Most are working hard to earn an honest crust. That said, there are a few real arseholes and there's not much you can do about them.

I'm proud to say that a lot of people I've worked with remain good friends. This includes union representatives, with whom I've had lengthy disagreements over the years - mostly when delivering difficult news, such as dismissals, redundancies and business closures. I've frequently been the face of bad news, bringing doom and gloom at Christmas when making job cuts or closing sites.

At one point, I earned the dubious soubriquet of 'The Smiling Assassin'. Despite this, I've always tried to treat people with dignity and respect and I have tried not to judge. I mean, just because someone takes a picture of their work colleague on the toilet and posts it on Facebook doesn't necessarily mean they are a bad person - they just did a daft thing.

Now, twenty-three years on from when this book is set and hopefully with many more years in HR to come, I've managed to persuade my friend J to help me put pen to paper. I'm here to take you on a guided tour of another world in a different time. A world that I grew up in, professionally speaking. This book starts right at the beginning of an HR career path in the 1990s, looking at life through the eyes of a green post-graduate in her first meaty HR role.

Our protagonist has had a soupçon of HR experience before this, but the time covered in this book is her first proper job in the industry. She is a rookie HR professional learning more on the job in live situations, faster than she could ever imagine, meeting some fantastic characters along the way.

So, please join me on this rollercoaster ride. Picture the Wild Mouse at Blackpool Pleasure Beach. You know, the one that was in its prime in 1986, lurching around corners like Evil Knievel on speed and supplying its riders with an unhealthy dose of whiplash.

This rollercoaster is not made of cold metal and

wood. It is a rollercoaster made up of people and their wonderful idiosyncrasies. Emotions. Flaws. Heartfelt warmth. Decisions, both good and bad. This book is about everyday people in all of their fabulous, humane, adventurous and slightly messed up glory.

By the way, the Wild Mouse at Blackpool has been closed down, but I hope you enjoy the journey on 'our girl's' HR equivalent.

'I'd tell all my friends, but they'd never believe me,
They'd think that I'd finally lost it completely.'
Radiohead – *Subterranean Homesick Alien* (1997)

Chapter 1

PLEASE TELL ME IT'S NOT ALL FERRETS AND ARSE CHEEKS!

It was a bleak November morning in Warrington - standard. As I walked along the pavement, the air hummed with the distant crackle of electricity pulsing through the wires. My own veins were coursing with adrenaline. My interview was imminent; mine was the final one before the panel would appoint. I was ready and hungry for it. I had just finished working for a large, well-known turf accountant and bookmaker; a wonderful den of iniquity where I learned how to gamble and identify syndicate match-fixing, alongside the basics of Human Resources and payroll. But this was something else; this interview could lead to the next big step in my career, working for and supporting some leading UK brands.

I was nervous because I desperately wanted the job. I liked everyone I had met so far, especially in the HR team. I thought it would be the type of business where I would learn a lot quickly, build up decent relationships and meet some interesting characters. I was not wrong.

Fast forward six hours, several in-tray exercises, numerous role plays, psychometric tests and interviews with the senior bods and I was called back into the interview room to be congratulated. I was told that my official start date would be January. Jan, who was my new boss, said she was looking forward to us working together. Tom, the MD, patted me on the back and said, 'Welcome on-board lass!'

'Obviously, you'll get a chance to meet everyone before then,' said Liz, who was an exuberant member of the interview panel. I could tell that she was going to be fun to work with. She had a 'no messing' streak to her character and a glint in her eye that smacked of mischief. 'You must come to the Christmas Party, December 22nd at Leigh Working Men's Club. I'll send you an official invitation. Gladys in 'Goods In' will sort you out with a ticket for the meat raffle.'

Excellent. I was over the moon. I have to admit that even now, a couple of decades later, the mere mention of a meat raffle gets me excited. You can take the girl out of Bolton, but you'll never take Bolton out of the girl! There was only one word for building up to meeting your new teammates properly, having to walk in solo and knowing they have probably been on the sauce all afternoon - trepidation. It turned out to be three words – 'Baptism of Fire'.

On the evening of December 19th, 1997, my boyfriend Matt gave me a lift to the party. He pecked me on the cheek, wishing me luck as he dropped me off. I had arrived promptly at the legendary Leigh

Working Men's Club, ready to ingratiate myself with my new work colleagues. Little did I know that I was to receive the warmest of welcomes, specifically two rather impressively pert arse cheeks squashed against the window next to the club's entrance. I'm not sure that I ever met the owners (who were apparently mooning for dares), but the welcome certainly didn't end there.

On entering the room, Tom Pringle, the MD, caught my eye, slid over and thanked me for making an effort to be there. 'It's good of you to come love. It'll be nice for you to meet people before your first proper day, although we might need you on duty should anything get out of hand. I think everyone's behaving so far though,' he said as he scanned the room nervously.

It certainly looked as though everyone was enjoying themselves. The room had that fun, upbeat Christmassy vibe to it - the one where everyone's merry and in the zone, just before things start to turn, like a lousy custard. Tom pointed out some of Harfield's key people who were giving it large on the dance floor. There was Ronnie, who was one of our most dedicated forklift truck drivers and an all-round nice bloke. Pamela Ainscough, who Tom described as 'the Li-Lo-Lil of Admin Ops, but nice enough.' I would find out why over the coming months. Keith and Paul, a couple of the warehouse lads, were leading the way with a small crowd jigging to 'Wig Wam Bam'. They were brothers

3

and had it nailed - you could tell they had led the dance charge many times before. Bob and Terry were there, along with their wives. They went out together most weekends and the four of them had synchronised jiving down to a tee. Tom introduced me to Sharon and the payroll team, which I would be managing on a daily basis. I'd briefly met Sharon during the interview process - she'd gone for the job too, so it would be interesting working with her and keeping her motivated. The team seemed friendly enough, at first glance, but I had a feeling Sharon's smile was through gritted teeth. Ah well, I like a challenge!

I asked Tom about the two chaps who were acting strangely and hovering around the main stage. John, one of the warehouse shift managers, was parading around the edge of the dance floor like an off-duty policeman, looking to nip any trouble in the bud before it arose. Apparently, he took his duties as a shift manager very seriously, even when not at work. His counterpart, Tony, caught my eye briefly. He was combing his silver hair in a pocket mirror for a good fifteen minutes before sidling up to various groups of unsuspecting women on the dance floor. They all gave him short shrift. He quite fancied himself as a bit of a ladies' man, even though his wife was sitting in the same space. She was helping herself to his hot pot supper as he prowled the room for his next unsuspecting victims.

Tom offered to buy me a drink before sliding

back to the management table and instructing me to come and join them. Of course, there would be a management table. God forbid any mingling with the masses at work-related social events!

Whilst I carefully scanned the room, looking for an HR table, I was suddenly accosted by a rather flamboyant 'Del Boy' type character, albeit with a bigger medallion. It was Paul Tetley and he definitely *wasn't* in the HR team. To quote directly, he didn't care 'two shiny shites about all that fluffy stuff, you know, like employment law'. He was the Transport Manager for two of the distribution centres. He took it upon himself to take charge of my initiation. He went into great detail about who was who, what they did for a living and whether or not, in his opinion, they were any bloody good. There were no boundaries to the cut of his jib and no filter. At all. Ever.

'Now then bonny legs!' were his first words to me, 'You're looking happy tonight. Did you get the pork sword before coming out or what?' I thought I'd misheard, but no. Words escaped me momentarily. As I started to mumble a response, he came straight back at me with 'Most people here have been neckin' it back all afternoon. You see her over there?' he asked, pointing to a smartly dressed lady in matching twin set and pearls sitting quietly hiccupping. I later came to know her as Lindsey, she ran the finance team. 'Works in accounts. Normally stiff as a dick, but today she's more pissed than my nan's mattress.' I wasn't too sure how to respond; either laughing with him, encouraging him or offending him. I needn't have worried because he was on a roll and he didn't stop for breath. 'You see him over there, dancing like a chicken? Well, he's not really dancing as such, he's got a bit of twitch. Well, I say a bit of a twitch, more like full onset Parkinson's disease. Unofficially obviously.' I looked over and saw a man happily grinding his way into a circle of ladies who were innocently dancing around their handbags. It was Tony Slater again. 'Watch out for him, love,' continued Paul. 'Bonnie lass like you, he'll be all over you like a three-peckered billy goat.'

Undeterred by my gaping mouth and lack of rhetorical banter, Paul continued. 'He's harmless, I suppose. I mean he's a bit of a shyster and a bit of a perve, but I think the truth is he does a lot a shaking-hands with the unemployed if you know what I mean!' he winked, pointing to his groin.

I thanked him for his insight and attempted to make my excuses to mingle with some of my other new workmates, but Paul was in full flow and having none of it. 'Have you seen the fucking comb-over on that? I mean he's alright, I suppose, but he's as bald as a roll-on deodorant underneath that thatch of hair and he goes puce with rage if you ever piss him off. Soon calms down, though.'

I looked over and saw that he was referring to his boss, our MD, Tom. Still unsure how to react, I simply over-emphasised my best 'non-pork sword' smile, nodded at him and started to edge away. Our paths crossed daily after this point and, as will become increasingly clear, the world through the eyes of Paul Tetley was a remarkable thing.

I made my way over to the obligatory management table, where everyone was really friendly to be fair. A few employees came over to make conversation and say hello to the new face in the room, which was nice. I was making the first steps towards getting to know my new colleagues. They were mostly happy drunks and all in all, I was pleased that I'd gone along.

I'd like to be able to say that the rest of the evening and my maiden voyage into the world of warehousing and distribution was uneventful, but that would be a hideous lie.

A couple of hours in, I looked in the direction of a small crowd that was gathering around a couple of tables. Two heavily built chaps were standing proudly on top of said tables performing a rousing rendition of 'Swing Low Sweet Chariot', filling a brief silence as the band handed over to the DJ for the rest of the night's entertainment. A loud clatter was heard as the two rugby players abruptly disappeared through the tables and crashed to the floor. I saw Tom negotiating payment with the bar manager and apologising profusely. It turns out that the two men in question were the union reps, Alex and Jason. They liked a party and I hoped this joyful outlook would bode well for our future relationship.

The customary punch up between employees followed, plus a precisely planned coup d'état attempt on members of the management team by shop floor employees after a lager top too many. There was only one broken jaw, two black eyes and a fractured nose, which was relatively mild; I'd seen worse. Less predictable was the fact that a convention of show ferrets was taking place in the hotel adjacent to the Club.

Just precisely how employees of Harfield Distribution happened to catch wind of the ferret convention is beyond me, but - catch wind of it they did. It seems that dares ensued involving four employees breaking into the function room, where the prize ferrets were being kept and setting them free. My understanding is that this was an act of drunken altruism rather than a statement in favour of ferret liberation, but what do I know?

In a flash, ferrets weaselled and war danced around each other, rolling over repeatedly with a chorus of hissing and squeaking. It was a festival for the feral and that was just the four inebriated employees. They quickly realised that liberating a busyness of wild ferrets wasn't one of the best ideas that they'd ever had. They were being bitten and nipped by the adorable, scratchy, sabre-toothed mammals and quickly decided to make for the nearest exits. A couple of members of the management team tried to pick up a few of the ferrets, but they were slippery little characters and smelt like someone had opened a grave.

It turns out that show ferrets can be quite expensive. You can pay tens or even hundreds of pounds for the right polecat - who knew? Well, the owners of said prize ferrets certainly did and were not best pleased when they found out what had happened. Unsurprisingly, everyone was asked to leave the Christmas do slightly earlier than planned. The negotiations that followed constituted my first HR job for the company - trying to appease the outraged hotel manager and his devoted concierge team. They had not expected to be having to hold the door for ferrets that night. They threatened to ban us from the club forever and call the police. We managed to persuade them that the fabulous foursome would be severely dealt with and we would help clear up any mess caused by their antics.

As it happened, it was ridiculously easy to identify the four men who had been victims of the ferret affray. A bit of blood, a lot of bragging and several casual enquiries about how to get a tetanus jab a couple of days after the event meant that we could narrow it down quite quickly. Those employees were dispatched to the hotel and club to do some cleaning and odd jobs, so all was good.

Back to that evening. It was almost locking up time at Leigh Working Men's club. The table clearing had been done; the ferret situation was under control and chairs had been stacked for the area to be cleaned in the morning - all except one. There was one solitary guy on a lone chair in the middle of the dance floor, Jason Wood. He'd had a crackin' night, culminating in dancing to 'Shang a Lang' with Julie from customer services and now he was fast asleep. He was suited, booted but slightly dishevelled with a slow-burning Marlboro Light hanging off his lips. Sensing danger, the remaining barmaid approached and tried to remove the carefully pursed ciggy from him. A defensive tussle erupted. It could be said that Jason was reluctant to comply with the help offered. Ten seconds later, he was asleep again on the chair, the ash burning away like a haggard old worm before dropping onto his once-white nylon shirt and setting him alight.

Within seconds, smoke alarms and sprinklers were activated. The intrepid barmaid rushed over to extinguish Jason. At that point, he stood up, uttered a disgruntled 'Fuck it!' as though someone had ruined his sweetest dream and not just saved his skin from a roasting. He promptly made his way home, remarkably unscathed.

So, 'baptism of fire' was accurate for that night in every sense of the phrase. It was a fabulous, realistic start to my induction with the business, providing a small taste of what was to come.

Chapter 2

Map Reading Is a Lost Art

Day one in the role. I was feeling anxious - the kind of nerves anyone has on the first day of a new job. I was hoping that no one would steal my dinner money or flush my head down the toilet (Grange Hill, circa 1983 during the Gripper Stebson years). For now, I had to walk the walk of fear through the warehouse to get to the HR office. Heads turned as people wondered who this woman was, dressed in her Joan Collins power suit and heels. Remember, it's the '90s. Luckily, friendly-faced Ronnie bounded up to me on his truck - all overalls and safety boots - and bestowed on me the warmest of welcomes.

'Hi, I'm Ronnie, I drive a forklift truck here, but at home, I have a Renault Espace and I take my family to Blackpool in it at the weekend. There's seven of us, so it's perfect, really!'

'Hi, nice to meet you. I'm Gemma and I'm starting a new job in HR.'

'You'll be grand, love. As long as you can listen to folk and you're not an absolute arsehole, you'll settle in really quickly,' he kindly coached. Wise words indeed.

Ronnie would greet me in the same friendly way every day for the next three years, minus the word 'arsehole'. As soon as he saw me coming, he'd sidle over on his truck to chat about what he had done at the weekend; or he'd ask how my evening was and whether I'd popped over to Blackpool at all for a midweek flurry on the 2p machines. Lovely guy who I suspect was a bit lonely at work. From then on, his presence made it a million times easier whenever I had to walk around the shop floor and speak to people, which was most days. There was *nothing* I didn't know about his Espace, seating capacity, transmission and even its MPG.

After a quick chat, off I trotted to the boardroom where the MD, Tom, introduced me properly to other members of the management team. First, there was Lindsey in Accounts who oozed stiffness. I could tell that she was super proud of her haughty, Daily Mail, black and white outlook on life. She had even dressed in monochrome. Then there was Liz in 'Supply Chain' who nodded at me in a decisive and probing way. She hunched up her very ample bosom and rested it on the board room table; both bazookas pointing at me, poised like trident torpedoes, ready to shoot me down should I say the wrong thing. I later learnt that Liz's bark (and her pointed nipples) were much worse than her bite.

Then there was John, one of the two warehouse managers. He looked constantly harassed and was persistently targeted by the MD for answers on performance figures. John's colleague and counterpart, Tony Slater, was quietly snoozing after a full week of nights. He'd been tracking down some troublesome potatoes, King Edwards, that had gone missing between warehouses in the vast logistics network of Great Britain. They had been located near Slough, much to Tom's relief and were now on their way to Scotland to be distributed to Pricetown stores over the border. Last but not least, let's not forget Paul Tetley who greeted me in true Paul Tetley style.

'Na' then sugar tits. Hope you've had plenty over Christmas because they're all ugly bastards around here!'

'Good morning to you too, Paul! Lovely to see you again,' I offered cheerfully. What else was the new kid on the block supposed to do? He couldn't phase me. No way, Jose!

Ninety minutes and lots of coffee later, I had my first Monday morning meeting under my belt. It was now time for me to meet Jan, my line manager and Regional HR Director. She came bounding in with six overflowing carrier bags of shopping and baby sick down her left lapel. 'Morning. Sorry I'm late, just had to drop the kids off in Preston, but you won't mind that will you? No? You are good! You'll have to come to visit them there with me one day; it's adorable. They have goats in the garden which we sometimes borrow for the weekend. We're thinking of getting a van especially and maybe adopting an ostrich too. Right, let's have a brew and get down to business, shall we?'

I think it was a directive rather than a question, but I liked Jan instantly. She was full of warmth and had a way of charming people into doing the right thing without them even realising it. A skill that I tried to emulate; it would prove invaluable over the years. She whisked me off into a different room to start my official induction process. Unbeknown to me, this alternative induction was to consist entirely of helping Jan to source, price and secure a brand-new caravan so that she could go away for weekends with her young family. Jan meanwhile, would be focusing on the crucial corporate objective of procuring a new tow bar for her Renault Laguna. She seemed pleased with my ability to navigate 'Auto Trader', so all was good.

By day two, I heard mention of some actual projects to which I was to be assigned. Some of them were familiar, fairly typical HR tasks such as helping the site to achieve the 'Investors in People' accreditation, offering NVQs and rolling out the appraisals system across all the regions that Jan looked after. She had a demanding job and a big team spread up and down the country. It was little wonder that she needed a caravan and weekend breaks to preserve some sanity. And, to be fair, this was the first time that I had been exposed to the sort of matrixed HR structure that had KPIs (Key Performance Indicators). There were management meetings based on metrics and data-based decision making. There was a lot to take in regarding structures and reporting lines, such as why Tom, who was overall MD, wasn't in charge of every function. But I was keen to learn and up for the challenge.

One of the more notable projects I looked after was the Driver Training Programme. At the time, there was a severe shortage of HGV drivers in the UK. This was a bit of an issue when your business model depended on drivers making deliveries. We created a plan to train some of the shop floor employees, mainly from the warehouse, but also from the wider business. The training would involve up-skilling operatives and office workers to obtain licenses to drive commercial HGVs. We called the programme 'Depot to Driving' and we were quite proud of how much interest it generated. I wanted the scheme to work and make a tangible difference to the business. I took a keen interest in all the participants to give them every chance of success.

Typically, it took between six and eight weeks to get an HGV licence. We decided that to be able to recruit and incentivise existing warehouse operatives to train as HGV drivers, we would backfill their jobs with agency workers. It seemed like a win-win situation. The transport department needed new drivers so that we could deliver to Pricetown stores on time. Warehouse operatives got the chance to re-train and double their income. My job was to organise the training, schedule it with the instructors we'd appointed from outside the business and identify the people who wanted to do it for the right reasons. It was crucial to do this before we made a significant investment in their training and development.

People applied through an internal advert and were interviewed by Paul Tetley and me. My first experience of Paul's distinguished selection skills involved him asking the interviewees 'So, why the actual fuck do you wanna do this? I hope to Christ it's not just for the money because I'll tell you now Sonny Jim (his universal address, regardless of gender) driving is no joke. You have to be with it, on your game, always thinking ahead and looking out for other knobheads on the road. So, we can't have any old Tom, Dick or Harry driving these massive fuckin' Class 1 lorries. Capiche?'

If our willing participants survived this rigorous process, the lucky ones embarked on an 'on the job' training programme. There would be four weeks shadowing drivers who were already in position, four weeks of driving alongside a designated driver trainer and, if they passed the test, a four-week trial period to check that things were hunky-dory. All the while, their permanent jobs were kept open so that our pioneers could return to their contracted roles if things didn't work out. It was a substantial investment on behalf of Harfield Distribution.

Every time someone 'graduated', my heart did a little jump for joy, just like a proud parent. However, in practice, the programme worked with varying degrees of success. Several participants passed with flying colours and to celebrate their achievements, we organised a mini graduation ceremony with certificate and licence presentations. We made a fuss of them and rightly so. They had shown significant commitment to train and learn skills for a completely different career. This positivity was crucial to the growth and future success of the business. Our ability to meet customer expectations was undoubtedly worthy of recognition. These people had taken a leap of faith and it had paid off. But of course, where people are concerned, things don't always go to plan. There are still a few exceptions.

Allow me to introduce Jack McGinty. Committed and dedicated as a warehouse operator. However, he occasionally lacked concentration. After weeks of training, the time came for him to embark on his maiden voyage from Warrington to Southport – a journey of precisely 30.1 miles. Paul and his team talked him through the key points; at the maximum recommended speed of 56.4 mph, the trip should take an average of one hour and two minutes when traffic would allow. This event was before Sat Nav, but every truck had a tachograph that tracked the journey. The statistics items captured for dissection included: time on the move, speed and rest breaks - rest breaks were a key legal requirement. It was a good job we had them installed. When Jack set off on his three-hour round trip, (this allowed an hour for goods to be unloaded at the Southport store) the tachograph was a helpful tool to understand where on God's green earth he'd been when he eventually returned, a whopping eight hours later!

I was gutted for Jack. He had been so keen to impress. However, an investigation had to be done. Who better to lead a sensitive investigation than the infamous Paul Tetley, master of understanding, empathy and diplomacy? I was there to keep the process on track, making sure that Jack was allowed to share any relevant points that he may wish to make. Just before the meeting started, Paul and I were prepping – Paul's unequivocal professional diplomacy already kicking in. 'I can't fucking wait for this!'

Attempting to coach Paul, I stressed the importance of allowing Jack to speak and give his version of events, being mindful of the embarrassment he would be feeling. So, just before Jack (visibly shaking) walked in with his union rep, I suggested that Paul should ask questions and perhaps listen more than he spoke, at least until we'd established all the facts. This would allow Jack to explain what had happened. Paul nodded his assent. In practice, however, my carefully chosen words seemed to fall on deaf ears.

I calmly opened the meeting, explaining that no one would be pre-judging anything. I went on to explain that we simply wished to get to the bottom of what had happened. Before I could properly finish my sentence, Paul took off his glasses and softly laid them on the table. He quietly rolled up his shirt sleeves as if preparing for fisticuffs, cracked his knuckles, looked John in the eye and started to speak in menacingly slow, Wigan dialect. 'First thing's first lad, pull yourself together. There's no need to be shaking like a shitting donkey on Blackpool pier. Now, can you tell me (long pause) why it took you (even longer pause, this time coupled with a sigh) *eight fucking hours* to drive from Warrington to Southport when I could have got there quicker walking with a fucking nail in my shoe?'

'I got lost. I just got lost and before I knew it, I was heading for Stranraer,' stuttered poor Jack.

'Stran-fuckin' raer! Are you having a giraffe? Did you not think you'd gone too fucking far when you saw signs for Preston, Lancaster, Morecambe, Kendal or Pen-fucking-rith? Did the bastarding penny not drop?'

Needless to say, Jack made a swift return to his warehouse duties, where apparently, 'it didn't fucking matter if he got lost amongst the bastard baked beans because at least there was a great big fucking wall at the end of each aisle to stop him going too fucking far. He could drive around in circles all friggin day if he liked!' Reluctantly, I had to admit that there was a logic to Paul's argument.

A trainee who had remarkably few difficulties along the way was Steve Luck - that said, never prejudge a name. He passed everything with flying colours - road traffic law and enforcement, fuel-efficient driving, load security, drivers' hours, walk around checks. You name it; he grasped it quickly. In short, we had no worries about him being on the road. However, looking back, he did ooze confidence which may have bordered on arrogance. One night, early in his driving career, he was bumbling his way around the Leeds inner-ring road on his way back from store deliveries. He'd had a long shift and was due to finish at 2.00 a.m. He came off the ring road a junction too early, ending up in a housing estate of Victorian terraced houses. The streets were narrow and tight, with parked cars peppering the kerbsides. In a panic to get back on the road and return to Warrington, it was fair to say that he was probably driving a tad too fast - his concentration perhaps not entirely on the job. At least that's what we told Mrs Gina Brown of East End Park, Leeds when she woke up with a start. Steve had carelessly driven the tractor unit of his 7.5-tonne truck directly into her living room. I mean to say, he didn't even use the front door! Despite Steve greeting Mrs Brown with a chirpy - and markedly inappropriate - 'Evening love, shall I put the kettle on?' this was not good 'luck' for Steve, Mrs Brown or Harfield Distribution.

The following day, the front page of the Yorkshire Post sported a rather embarrassing headline: 'A whole new meaning to Pricetown's Home Delivery Service'. The journalist responsible for the evening edition had a field day with this. The headline read 'Smashing New Home Drop Off Solution From

Pricetown - You Shop, They Drop… a truck into your front room!' It didn't look much better on Look North, come to think of it. Or on Granada Reports. Or in the local papers, every night for a week. Or the snippet that was shown repeatedly on the 10 o'clock news across all channels. Thank the Lord it was in the early days of mobile phones and internet coverage as it was hard enough keeping a low profile about it. Every few minutes reporters called the HR Department for an official company viewpoint. Part of our role was to be the appointed media contact in a crisis. There is a limit to the number of 'no comment' or 'I'm so sorry, but I'm unable to give you any details about the incident' statements available before you become bored of your own voice. Suffice to say, Steve made a swift return to his previous role - another beautiful driving career thwarted by little things getting in the way, like houses.

Then there was Brian who had worked in the warehouse for over twenty-five years before taking the plunge into HGV driving. Lovely chap, who'd married his childhood sweetheart, Elsie and had five daughters with her. I'm not sure if it was a sign of a warped affection or complete and utter laziness on his part, but each of his daughters had a number rather than name. Conversations would go something like:

'Morning Brian, good weekend?'

'Hectic, love. Number one brought her three

around for two sleepovers, number four is up the duff again and number five's boyfriend has just gone down for benefit fraud, leaving her and us with his three kids. So, I'm knackered and skint, but then again, it keeps the wife busy.'

'Bet you wouldn't swap it though?'

'No love. They're all good fun, but I'm still thinking of cashing in my pension for a one-way ticket to Benalmadena. A single, obviously.'

'Right. Well, best of luck with the training today. Are you sure you're ok to drive with all that going on?'

'Yes love, I'm fine thanks. Tough as old boots me and raring to go! It's keeping me sane this driving job.'

So, Brian would climb into his machine and set off for the day with his trainer by his side, motivated by the need to earn more money and retire abroad – ideally, if possible, by the end of the following week. For the most part, Brian was a safe pair of hands. Steady away, nothing crazy, just thorough and patient, if a little tired. I say for the most part because we were a little bamboozled when we got a call from the Wiltshire police force, reporting that Brian and his truck had mounted the infamous magic roundabout in Swindon causing a gargantuan traffic backlog across the area.

Now, this roundabout was not a mini-roundabout that you could skirt around. No. This beast was huge - a gyratory in its own right with a forest in the middle of it. You'd have to be registered blind or have a well thought out suicide plan to drive into it at 30 mph. Brian's story was that the sun was in his eyes. I knew that this was a mistake as soon as the words had left his mouth.

'Bollocks!' said Paul Tetley during the follow-up investigation. 'Have you never heard of shades, or sunglasses or Reactolite fuckin' Rapides? Or maybe a fuckin' baseball cap? What about preparation, man? Would you go out in fuckin' speedos if it was snowing? Or wear a jumper in the fuckin' desert? Jesus Christ, my four-year-old grandson, could work out that you need sunglasses to drive when it's fuckin' sunny!'

That was the end of another beautiful driving career. We strongly suspected that Brian had nodded off for a few seconds - obviously at the wrong moment. This theory was further compounded when he returned to his warehouse job and had been found having a mid-shift kip in one of the loos on more than one occasion. Either that or he didn't know the difference between his number ones, number twos and his siestas - poor fella.

We didn't give up though; the majority of interested employees passed the training programme with flying colours. I quite enjoyed donning my hi-vis vest, watching them practise reverse parking in the transport yard and, on occasion, going with them to make a delivery to a local store. I got a lot from this (and still do) as I learnt more about the challenges and opportunities that drivers face during their regular shift. It wasn't much fun driving in the snow at 3.00 a.m. only to find that the guy at the store who was meant to be helping unload the truck had been put on alternative duties. In this case, the Harfield driver would have to jump out of the truck and unload the goods himself, often getting soaked and cold before continuing the rest of his shift. If you were lucky and the store was modern, it might have a canopy or integrated 'goods-in-loading / unloading bay' so that you didn't get quite so drenched. However, more often than not, the stores were old. You just had to utilise the tiny space you had to get close to the door and get the goods in, before continuing the rest of your shift cold, wet and hungry.

Going out with the drivers, working a shift in the warehouse freezer and 'walking a mile' in the employees' shoes helped me gain a valuable insight into things. Undoubtedly, I had a better appreciation of the difficulties that employees faced when they were simply trying to get the job done. I've always tried to do this wherever I've worked. This way, you can relate to things from the employee's perspective when things go wrong and help other managers understand things that might not be immediately obvious. It also helps massively with engagement and retention when you can help to fix problems quickly.

My induction continued in a similar vein. I went

to meet Jan for a review of my probationary period - an evaluation of my time in the role so far. We were to discuss what had gone well, what targets I should work on, what to focus on in the coming months and any areas for development. As the meeting drew to a close, she simply said, 'Work wise you're doing fine, but the real test is at the weekend. We're heading for Bognor in the caravan, so if you've picked the right one for my tow bar, you're a keeper!'

Twenty years on, we're still friends and colleagues. She was the best line manager I've ever had - before or since. I learned so much from her in terms of approach, style and how not to be judgemental. I was a rookie, I made mistakes, but instead of a Spanish Inquisition, Jan would simply say, 'Bet you won't do that again, will you?' which held firm every time.

Some HR people think they're special; they abuse the control or power that they have by dint of being privy to certain information and being in the 'inner circle' of trust. Contrary to all that nonsense, Jan trusted her team until someone gave her reason not to. Then they would know about it. It was a great team in which good working relationships and lifelong friendships were formed. Jan had a fabulous sense of humour and a warm laugh that would engulf her whole body, drawing in everyone around her. Her character generated colossal trust. As our leader, we would walk through walls for her to get things done the right way. She was a master of killing people with kindness, but with a core of steel running through her, the truth would always come out in a difficult negotiation or investigation. People would instinctively open up to her and this is just what you need in order to get to the bottom of an issue or concern. I've always admired that particular skill. In short, Jan had a 'hearts and minds' leadership style and I've tried to emulate that throughout my career. Even when you have to be tough and strong, deliver difficult news or toe the company line, there's no need to be an arsehole about it. Simple.

And right now, Jan is helping me to pick a caravan (and tow bar!) for *my* family. Can't wait to go to Bognor and check it out.

Chapter 3

MANAGEMENT UNION RELATIONS AND UNOFFICIAL BARBECUES

One thing to mention early doors is the fact that the business was highly unionised. At each site, the split between salaried and hourly paid employees was probably in the region of 75% blue-collar, shop floor, hourly paid employees to 25% office based, salaried staff. Shop floor roles included picking items to order, packing them into cages (which looked a bit like the concierge trolleys you see in big hotels) and loading the lorries which would then deliver the goods to the stores. There was a hierarchy amongst these roles and woe betide anyone who tried to mess with it. For example, the pickers and packers who worked in the freezers were paid more than those in the ambient warehouse. The people who worked in admin operations were paid more than people in the warehouse. However, if you had a forklift truck licence, you were basically 'God of the Shop Floor'.

Next up in the pecking order were the transport guys, the lorry drivers who were paid more than anybody because of the increased level of responsibility that they carried on the road. It reflected the value of the transportation of goods and the hideous shifts that they worked. After all, there can't be many less glamorous jobs than arriving in Runcorn at 6.00 p.m. on a cold January night with five tonnes of frozen food to unload before you could settle down to your 'cuppa soup'.

Almost everyone in these roles was a member of the recognised union on-site, the T&G (Transport and General Workers Union). The union represented their members for collective bargaining purposes, covering annual pay negotiations, changes to terms and conditions, shift patterns and overtime rates. They also accompanied their colleagues into the grievance and disciplinary meetings, automatically taking their side, no matter the size or nature of misdemeanour that they may, or may not, have committed. It wasn't uncommon for an employee's representative to ask for a quick word before a meeting and say, 'Look, I know Sam has been caught on camera pissing all over the Golden Delicious, but he was desperate. I have to defend him love, that's my role, what can I do?'

Privately, I often wanted to encourage the rep to say that his colleague (or 'member' as they were affectionately known) had a severe medical condition, compulsive disorder or bladder control problem. As long as they owned up, showed remorse and never repeated the misdemeanour, they might get away with a warning and keep their job. Occasionally, I would have a word on the quiet to give a bit of guidance on how an employee needed to play things if they wanted to keep their job, as long as the rep in question was sound and the employee was otherwise ok.

One such rep was Alex Gataki. A towering colossus of a man; huge in every sense of the word. Big guy physically, prodigious personality and a huge influencer when it came to galvanising people and getting them on-side. He was a natural leader and I learned very quickly that gaining Alex's trust meant getting things done quickly and in the right way. If he wasn't 'on-side', then things just didn't happen as smoothly. Luckily, he was fair-minded, kind-natured and had a tonne of common sense. More often than not, where there might be a fundamental disagreement about a new way of working or how their supervisor was treating a member, we'd sort things out over a brew in the canteen and reach an agreement before things escalated.

One example was during an unexpected spring heatwave when there was a massive rush on orders for meat and garden furniture on a particular Easter bank holiday weekend. One of the warehouse managers, Tony Slater, had barked at an entire shift that they needed to cancel their plans for the weekend and 'work like Billio because orders won't ship themselves!'. Here was the response to a motivational command from Tom that 'the nation has asked for sausages and we shall give them sausages! Sort it out, Tony. Our country needs us!'

Tony was not exactly 'Mr Popular' with his team. They felt he had an arrogance about him;

telling people what to do rather than asking them; instructing rather than supporting; speaking down to people rather than encouraging and uplifting them. As a result, there was no goodwill in the tank when Tony needed a favour from his team. He frantically went around the shifts ordering, dictating and pronouncing that they must work overtime at the weekend to fulfil demand.

Overtime was optional rather than compulsory, although most employment contracts stated that people needed to work a *reasonable* amount to get the job done. Despite Tony's best (or worst) efforts, he could not get people to work. In desperation, he came to see me ahead of an emergency management meeting called by Tom. Asking for help from a colleague did not sit well with Tony's ego. His natural starting point was to blame the workforce.

"Lazy, ungrateful bastards!" He shouted as he entered my office, throwing some paperwork down on the table, fiddling with his tie and twitching slightly, as he was prone to do.

"Who would that be then, Tony?" I asked casually, knowing full well that our very own Mr Motivator was likely to have failed in his mission to engage the people we needed to work a full weekend of additional hours.

"These operators. They won't do it. They just won't work. Absolute arseholes the lot of them. Tom is gonna go mental in a minute when I tell him." He was worried.

"Have you asked them to work?" I said.

"Course I bloody have. Have you not been listening?" he stressed.

"Yes, but have you?' He looked confused. 'Have you *asked* them, or have you *told* them to work?"

"What difference does that make?" he yelled.

"Well, a massive difference actually, Tony. Often, it's not *what* you say; it's *how* you say it. If you asked me to work as a favour, acknowledged the sacrifice that I'd be making by not seeing my own family on the warmest day of the year, said you'd be very grateful on behalf of the business and paid me double bubble, I'd probably do it for you. However, if you barked at me, told me I had to do it (when I know full well that I don't) and called me an ungrateful bastard, I'd make sure that I wasn't available to work. *That's* the difference. So, what have you said and how did they respond?" He looked puzzled but, before he could reply, Paul Tetley knocked on the door, opened it swiftly and told us that Tom was ready for the management meeting to start. More accurately, he opened the door, belched and said, "Now then knobheads. Time for a kickin' if your shit's not sorted for the weekend!" Galvanising, to say the least.

We entered the boardroom and awaited the arrival of Tom. Jan was already in there and asked me how it was looking in terms of people for extra weekend shifts. "A bit of a mixed response," was all I could offer at this stage.

Tom eventually entered the room - or rather flung the door open - and, with a profusion of sweat on his brow, implored his team to tell him that we had adequate cover in all operational areas for the weekend. He cut straight to the chase.

"Pricetown is chomping at the bit and my cock is firmly on the block if we can't fulfil this demand. Liz - is admin sorted?" he asked.

"Yes, Tom - all sorted. We can print most of the work tickets this afternoon and tonight, so we'll just need a half a dozen in tomorrow and a skeleton staff on Sunday. I've got the rota here if you want to go through it. I'll be checking in myself over the weekend." Perfect. That's what you want to hear as an MD; a manager in control of her workload, her people, committed to work and everything good to go, especially when your private parts are up for grabs, so to speak.

"Good work. Thanks, Liz," said Tom, looking a little more relaxed. "Paul, how many drivers have we got?"

"90% covered Tom. No issues with anyone working extras. I've got four more to call today after 2.00 p.m. as they were on nights yesterday, but I don't foresee any problems. If there are any gaps, Alan and Danny have offered to go back driving for the weekend. All in all, consider it covered."

I was impressed. When the chips were down, Paul could pull it out of the bag. Alan and Danny were two of his supervisors - former drivers who had recently been promoted, so it was good to hear that they were willing to make deliveries if we needed them.

"Brilliant. That's good. Thanks Paul. So, all we need now is a few warehouse operatives to step up which should be fairly straightforward, given how many we can ask, right Tony?" he asked, hopefully.

Tony twitched, played with his tie, looked at the floor, tapped his pen on the desk and mumbled, "I'm struggling Tom. I can't get them to work." Tom's pallor changed briskly from slightly red to puce - it didn't take long. Paul Tetley coughed and caught my eye, willing me to witness the pressure cooker explode.

"What do you mean Tony? Have we got enough people to fulfil this massive request for our biggest, no wait, ONLY customer, or not? Please tell me that you've managed to do your job and get people to work!"

"Erm, well, not exactly," started Tony.

"What do you mean? We need thirty people over the weekend, how many have you got?" demanded Tom.

"Well, there's a couple…" said Tony unwisely.

"A couple?' said Tom incredulously. 'A bloody couple? That's as much use as tits on a fish!!" he exclaimed in true Paul Tetley style. Paul stifled a giggle at this point. "Given that your department, the warehouse, is the biggest department and we have shed loads of agency workers in that area,

how can it be that you have only found two willing
people to work?"

"Well, apparently they're all going to the same
barbecue, so none of them can work," he said.

"Well, I hope they're not thinking of shopping
at Pricetown coz there'll be fuck all food in stock,"
muttered Paul under his breath. Tom heard him and
didn't smile. Great, I thought. Unofficial industrial
action. Just what we needed.

"Tony, that's pathetic. Everyone else in this room
has managed to get things covered and all you have
is excuses. How has it got to the point where they
won't work for you? There's only one thing for it,"
said Tom as he turned to face me. He uttered the
following immortal words that stayed with me for
the rest of my career. "Gemma, you're in charge
of morale. You need to meet with Alex and the
other reps and sort this out - pronto!" Tony looked
relieved, temporarily.

"Tony, you come with me. We need to talk,"
said Tom. With that, he blustered out of the door
as quickly as he had come in. Tony shuffled
uncomfortably before standing to leave.

"Six of the best for you, lad!" said Paul, smiling
at Tony.

"Piss off!" replied Tony, grumpily, knowing
full well that he was about to have a difficult
conversation with the boss. I turned to Jan and,
given my new elevation to Chief Morale Officer,
told her I was off to find the reps. "Do you want

me to come with you?" she offered, but I wanted to stand on my own two feet and try to turn this around. There was only one way I knew and that was to be completely candid with the union reps who had an excellent nose for bullshit. I went to find Alex first, knowing that if I could persuade him about the cause, others might follow. I got Alex a cold drink from the vending machine and asked him what was going on.

"Don't look at me. Everyone in our department is working," Alex said. As a driver for the business, that much was true.

"Come on," I said, "You must know what's going on in the warehouse. Why are they all suddenly at a barbecue and unavailable for work?"

"Just the way it goes, I suppose," he said casually.

"Level with me, Alex. Just tell me how it is. I think I have an idea, but I want to hear it from you."

"Well, in case you didn't know, they won't work any more than they have to for Tony Slater. Every day of every year he's an overbearing, condescending prick to them and this is the one chance that they have of getting even with him. Most people bite their tongues day in day out, but they've been waiting for this moment; it's a rare opportunity to flip the bird at him. I reckon you could offer to pay them in gold bullion and they would still tell Tony to shove his overtime where the sun doesn't shine."

"Right." I nodded, now understanding the task entirely. "So, what do you think it would take to persuade people?"

"Not sure you can. It's not about money or anything like that. It's a long-awaited chance for revenge. I think we should speak with Jason though because the warehouse is his patch. See what he says?"

"That's fine," I agreed, "but before we do, I need to know that you'll help me persuade him that we need people to work. It's important for all of us that we meet the customers' expectations, or they might go elsewhere and that's not good for any of us. We need to avoid that if we can. I understand the point that people are making and that will be looked into, but I would hate for this to backfire into something that none of us would want to happen." Luckily, Alex understood and said he would do his best if we could see Jason together.

Jason was ok too to be fair. He was a bit of a maverick and his thought processes were somewhere between numb and genius. Jason had a sharp tongue, glasses so thick you couldn't cut them with a laser and a frightful temper. He could go from singing, 'Good morning, good morning to you', in an operatic fashion whilst bringing you a brew, to threatening to hit someone 'with a cudgel' in a nanosecond. I'd never heard the word 'cudgel' before meeting Jason. I had to look it up. It was not associated with good things.

So, I bought Jason a cold drink too. He was in relatively good spirits for a man prone to referencing medieval weaponry in everyday conversation. I asked what the problem was with the request to work at the weekend. He said in very plain English that Tony Slater was a 'twat and hell will freeze over before people work the weekend for him'.

Good to know. "What do you think it would take for people to change their minds, Jason? There must be something?"

"Nothing really," he said. "But I think it might help if Tony was to beg," he offered, with a grin on his face.

Ah, now we had it. Temporarily glossing over the fact that the reps wanted a senior manager of the business to plead with them to work, I could sense that there was hope. There was no way that Tony would beg and no way I would ask him to - it was blackmail after all. But it wasn't my job to make things worse, so I had to appeal to Jason's better nature. Luckily for me, he wasn't without intelligence.

"The thing is Jason, it's not just about one-upmanship at a time like this. If we don't work, we're biting the hand that feeds us. If we don't do it, Pricetown will find somewhere that will. If we have to rely on agency workers this weekend, then who's to say that won't become the norm? You guys won't get the chance to earn as much in the future as you have been doing. There's a bigger picture here and it goes beyond Tony Slater." I offered.

"She's right, mate," said Alex. "I've worked

in other places where this has happened and the regular, full-time workers just got frozen out for overtime after a while. We don't want that here, pal; it should be us creaming the overtime first."

"Yep, I know," said Jason, thinking cap firmly in place. "Look, I can talk to people. I think I can get them to see what's at stake and work the weekend, but you are going to have to sort Tony out. He's a liability, winding people up when he doesn't need to. He talks to people like they are something he has stood in and then demands respect from them - it doesn't work like that. So, I'll talk to people, but don't think that this won't happen again as long as that twitching dick head is in charge."

I thanked Jason, promised to speak with Tony and reminded him not to mock the afflicted. I asked if he would give me an update in thirty minutes after he had had a chance to speak with people. Alex offered to go with Jason to talk with the employees who were on shift. I said that I could go along too if it would help, but they wanted to give it a go on their own first. I left them to it and went to find Tom, who was in his office, pacing the floor and still tearing strips off Tony. I explained that there seemed to be a problem with the way that Tony spoke to people, which was why there was a reluctance to work. I added that the union reps were negotiating with people now, to try and convince them to do the overtime. I told Tom what I'd said to them and that, if we did manage to get the numbers,

I thought it would help if Tony and other people on the management team could thank them personally.

"No way!" said Tony defiantly. "They've proper embarrassed me today. There's no way I'm thanking any of the little bastards!"

I opened my mouth to speak, but before I could say anything, Tom did the job for me. He explained to Tony that this was not about him, adding in no uncertain terms that he *would* be getting out there to thank people. To make it easier, Tom would accompany him to make sure that Tony did it correctly, as Tom would be expressing his gratitude too. To be fair, Tom did get out into the operational areas quite a bit and people respected him for that. Him going around the different departments to thank people would not have been too out of the ordinary.

Just then, Alex and Jason arrived giving us the news that we wanted to hear. We had just enough warehouse cover for the weekend. I learned that Ronnie was the first to sign up after hearing that I'd had a chat with the reps, which was heart-warming. I thought Tom would shake their hands, but instead, he offered them a big bear hug. I thanked them and said we appreciated the time they had taken to do this. We would get around the shop floor areas to thank people too. Tony managed to mutter a thank you with zero eye contact.

So, the weekend shift ran, orders were fulfilled and the customer was none the wiser. I suggested to Tom that we should order pizza in for people's lunch breaks and put the vending machines on free for the weekend. After initially saying that he was in no position to splash the cash, he reluctantly agreed. It went down well. Both Alex and Jason said it was a nice touch and so, on we went.

I kept reminding Tom that we needed a robust plan B when it came to fulfilling weekend overtime. As much as I understood the employees' point of view, the operation could not be held to ransom like that. I also pointed out that we ought to dig deeper into Tony's management style and remind him how this whole episode could have ended up differently. However, he was so relieved to get the job done that he didn't want to open up the inevitable can of worms that these types of conversations could uncover. Ultimately though, he knew that something would have to change. As Tony's line manager, this had to be driven by him when he was ready. He did agree with me that Tony should sit in on the monthly management union meetings. I wanted him to see things from the employee's point of view and, I figured life would be more comfortable if Tony and his troops could build a better relationship. This theory worked - to a point. Usually, they would argue and bicker quite a lot, but that just made the job of stepping in and finding middle ground easier for me to achieve. It was hard work on occasions, but I think it helped as all parties had to accept that they needed to work together to achieve their objectives.

For the most part, we continued to operate like this. When really serious situations arose, Alex would ask the regional officer of the Transport and General Workers Union to come on-site: a full-time official, whose salary was paid for by the members. Naturally, it was in their best interests to act on behalf of the shopfloor workers and support them, no matter what the situation. That said, a good regional officer could help get things over the line as long as they could demonstrate why it was necessary and that there was a logic behind the decision-making process. A weak regional officer could often be a hindrance and put blockers in place to stop things from happening. As a general rule, I set time aside to build relationships with local and regional representatives, giving them updates on the business as often as I could. This way, they knew what was going on and when someone made big announcements, there were no nasty surprises. Being at loggerheads was never a helpful place to be and throwing your weight around would only provide a definitive path to a stalemate. So, trust and integrity were vital and if the canteen coffee didn't work, then a pie and a pint down the pub usually did.

Regional officers were also invited to accompany locally-elected union representatives to discipline and grievance meetings. As trusted members of the workforce trained in all things relating to health and safety, conduct and behaviour, you would hope that union reps and disciplinary situations were few and far between. It was, therefore, something of a surprise when Jason was reported for allegedly patrolling the site one night on a swivel chair. Something that only came to light after he plunged from the mezzanine roof onto several pallets of Jersey Royals.

To be fair to Jason, he was pretty straightforward and honest about the whole thing. However, this didn't prevent the usual posturing from Bobby Buck, the union's regional officer. After hobbling into the meeting room on crutches, Jason tried to place them neatly at the side of his chair, at which point they crashed down, landing just short of Bobby's feet. Bobby gave John and me a fifteen-minute sermon. Bobby covered how this incident was completely out of character, how we ought to consider all of the excellent work that Jason did; both as a warehouse operative and as a representative, not to mention how he single-handedly resolved the bank holiday weekend problem. After all this, Jason simply added, "Yep, I did that. We were a bit bored on nights, so I thought I'd put the time to good use and have a look round the site for predators and intruders. As it goes, I didn't find either and I know I should have walked rather than going around on a chair, but I'd twisted my ankle playing golf earlier in the day. It wasn't bad enough to be off sick, so I thought I'd come and put a shift in."

"And why did you feel the need to patrol the site

when we have 24/7 security?" I asked, "And what predators have you ever seen roaming around?"

"Well, I take my union duties very seriously and see the security of this site as part of my remit. There had been reports of a strange wolf-like creature prowling around the area. It's been seen around the back of Burger King at Haydock services, so you can't be too careful. I was poised, ready to defend this site and all who work here with my trebuchet," he said with pride. I gave him a quizzical look, a 'mum look', trying to convey 'don't take the piss'. Luckily, he twigged.

"Alright... I was bored and Kevin Docherty bet me a tenner to do it. Would have been fine if I hadn't lost control of my vehicle and fallen through the bannister. That said, a trebuchet would be a handy addition to our security!" he mused.

"Right. Well, thanks for being honest. Next time leave the patrolling duties to Security and if you must wander around, do us a favour and walk. It cost a bloody fortune to replace that barrier. And next time you get caught red-handed, spare us the bullshit. Better still - don't get caught," concluded John.

"Even better than that, don't do it in the first place," I added.

"Understood," said Jason sheepishly. He was let off with a warning and all was well with the world. Some managers would have taken great joy in making an example of a union rep. I know every business requires rules, but no need to use them as weapons - medieval or otherwise - if you don't have to.

Good working relationships between the management team, the union representatives and their 'members' (still makes me smile!) were crucial to achieving objectives. Being available for a chat, conducting meetings respectfully and listening to the union's point of view, meaning that we all realised we were working towards the same goal. Ultimately, the aim was to keep the business going, offer job security and keep costs low.

This policy was particularly true when conducting annual wage negotiations. For the first couple of years at Harfield, it was a serious affair. It was Lindsey in accounts' job to tell me, in a pinched tone, that we had a 2% maximum budget for the hourly paid groups - no more. During the negotiations, I had to 'sell it' and get a deal with the union and the people they represented. For Lindsey and her department, it was all about budgetary control. It always irked me that I had no influence over the arbitrary amount given to me, nor did the accounts department have to sit in on the meetings and try and negotiate a deal. I just had to make sure that I got a 2% agreement (or less) and not a penny more!

By way of preparation, it was my job to produce a report about the local and national economic conditions, the impact of planned minimum wage increases and to show what our local competitors were paying in the area. I would then present this information to the union rep, whilst sucking my teeth and explain that things were tough out there. In the spirit of negotiation, we would then offer a derisory 0.5% as a starting point, for them to come back to say it was insulting and ask for 10%. We would then call the 10% ridiculous and, after a week or two, we would usually agree on 2%, which was better than nothing.

The format for the annual negotiations remained the same. I would lead on behalf of the business and there would usually be one other member of the senior management team with me to show solidarity. Obviously not Lindsey, who never wanted to get her hands dirty, which was fine; I don't think she would have helped anyway.

Eventually, we did get to the point where Alex, Jason, their counterparts in other departments and I could have an honest, open conversation. Being frank, I could say during the first meeting, 'This year's budget is 2% owing to X, Y and Z. We can't go above that; we can spend a couple of weeks dancing around it and pissing up each other's backs with proposals, or we can just agree on it now and have an early finish.' After a minute's pause and a quick chat amongst themselves, they usually agreed. This approach was acceptable unless there was zero budget. In this scenario, more time and thought would be required to explain the economic climate and the reasons why occasional pay freezes had to be implemented.

In terms of day-to-day activity, the local, on-site union reps were pivotal to everything we did. They either had an open and overt role to play in things like negotiations, redundancies, changes to terms and conditions of employment and representing their members in discipline and grievance situations or, a more subtle role, helping disseminate important messages.

We set up monthly management/union meetings with the reps on-site and invited the regional officers such as Bobby in for a chat. Such gatherings were mostly out of courtesy, but fostering the relationship was massively helpful when colleagues faced difficult, more challenging decisions. These often took place at the pub over dinner and a pint. I met with the local reps, like Alex and Jason, on-site almost daily and even if there wasn't much to talk about, I made an effort to get to know more about them, their families and pastimes. In this way, official meetings ran more smoothly.

Some businesses I've worked with were reluctant to foster good relationships with unions, especially the US-owned ones where 'Teamster' style activity-filled them with fear. My take on it is that management/union relationships can be beneficial when appropriately conducted. It all starts and ends with communication. I can't overstress the importance of getting these relationships right.

All things considered, I was pleased to have Alex, Jason and the other reps to work alongside. They were decent people and we got stuff done, even if this did involve the odd trip to the White Hart and a pack or two of Nobby's Nuts!

Chapter 4

A Day in the Life Of...

To give you an idea of the size and scale of the distribution centres where I worked, they employed eight hundred people each on average. Jan looked after five of the sites situated between Livingstone and Bournemouth. She, therefore, depended on her team to crack on and keep her posted on the major issues; Jan trusted us, we trusted her, it all worked.

The HR teams on site were responsible for payroll, recruitment, contracts, maintaining strong employee relations with the union, training and development along with any restructuring or redundancies that needed attention. It was a busy old role but hugely fulfilling. The only way to do justice to the service we provided was to have regular meetings, every day, week, month, to make sure we were all dancing to the same tune. For the HR teams; due to location, this was mostly by phone and, occasionally, face to face. It was a great example of remote communication and way ahead of its time.

Dawn and I both reported to Jan and we spoke to or met each other every day. The sites were run in unison and were geographically close together. Certain meetings were standardised, such as daily production, weekly payroll, absence reviews, management/union meetings the list goes on. These were non-negotiable, admin-heavy meetings and processed data that reached the highest echelons of Harfield Distribution. They happened with the same cadence every time, so much so that it was impossible not to become accustomed to patterns and nuances in everyone's behaviours, appearance and speech. The weekly management meeting, designed to form an overview from all department heads, was included; a way of keeping everyone in the loop.

Cue the re-entry of Tony Slater, the operations manager whose silver-fox hair would glisten and gleam under the bright tungsten glare of warehouse strip lighting. Tony, clearly in the throes of a mid-life crisis, had decided to take radical action. He walked in, obviously nervous but trying to act casually, sporting his new chestnut brown hair colour. As I said before, the meetings were regular, so, his esteemed colleagues quickly spotted Tony's new barnet hue. We exchanged surreptitious glances, but nothing more than that initially. Tony felt he was in safe territory. Tony felt his colleagues had accepted that his once greying hair, was now a shiny Chocolate Labrador colour. He didn't spot the silent tongue biting and the odd mouthed exchange of 'what the fuck?' between his peers.

"Something different about you, Tony?" asked Tom, with no hint of irony.

"No, I don't think so Tom," said Tony casually, "shall we make a start?"

Fast forward forty-five minutes and Liz was chairing the section on building improvements. This part of the agenda had been planned and underway for some time. Discussions began on new colours for the canteen walls; a plethora of options - from Egg Nog Tan to Periwinkle Purple but after much deliberation and a short pause, she declared, "Personally, I've always been partial to a rich brunette colour you know, like pedigree dog shit," the laughter started there.

"Jesus Christ! I knew if anyone was going to comment, it would be you, Liz. You just couldn't let it lie, could you?"

From that point onwards, nobody could keep up with the remarks about 'Just For Men' and 'Grecian 2000'. Tony earned the new nickname of Bisto Bonce.

"Show us your new tattoo, Tony," said Liz next. "You really are a stud muffin now sunshine, with your new tat and youthful hairdo! The ladies are queuing up for you, son!"

"Oh no, be quiet, Liz, I told you that in confidence," said Tony grouchily.

"Well, it's an open secret love. I know at least three of the girls from the Rochdale store have seen it in the flesh!" she offered.

"Bloody hell," said Tom, raising his hand to his brow whilst the rest of us sat intrigued.

"No. No way. Some things are best left private," said Tony, twitching more than ever, visibly anxious about the impending revelation.

"Well, I think you should live and let live. It's up to you what you have imprinted about your person. But you're amongst friends Tony and there's nothing wrong with having 'Blow the horn' tattooed just below your belly button with an arrow pointing towards your todger, nothing at all. And it's proving to be a winner with the ladies, isn't it?" said Liz in full flow.

"Jesus Christ!" said Tony. "Can't a man have any secrets around here?"

But he was smiling and it was quite funny. I think he was quite proud of his conquests and was enjoying the attention. Despite the small detail that Tony was allegedly happily married and three of the employees in one of our customer's stores were very well acquainted with his body art. I made a mental note that we should probably address that at some point. There was always a difficult conversation waiting in the wings where Tony was concerned.

All of that aside, the camaraderie amongst that team of people was excellent, but no one was immune to having the piss ripped out of them. It just happened to be Tony's turn. The professionalism in meetings was there somewhere, but it could be difficult to track and colleagues often crossed the boundary lines. It certainly didn't take much to throw meetings off course.

In fact, this was the first environment where I'd been invited to play 'Buzzword Bingo' or 'Wank

Bingo' as Paul liked to call it. He'd even gone to the trouble of printing everything out on bingo cards for us and handing them around to everyone but Tom. He was prepped and ready to shoot.

In the overall scheme of things, Tom was pretty straight-talking, but we could always tell when he'd been in meetings or on away days with Pricetown. He turned into a proper corporate animal when he got back to Warrington. Gradually, we'd start to pick up (and, to our mortal shame occasionally use) some of the terms that had become part of Tom's indoctrination.

"Working for the market leader in retail is a great honour, but can have its challenges," he'd say. "It was great to touch base with Pricetown this week, identify the low-hanging fruit in the food retail sector and understand some of the reasons behind the paradigm shift in their approach to the market. We can't rest on our laurels though, that's crystal clear. We need to be on our toes, step it up a level, right across the board. Every department in our business needs to be on their game. As one of Pricetown's major partners in the supply chain cycle, we need to take a 'Customer First' approach and show them that we too can think outside the box, push the envelope and float our ideas. It's time for some blue-sky thinking. Let's walk the walk and talk the talk. We can do this, people!"

Things would continue in this way until one of Tom's valued team members shouted 'Bingo!' He went along with it at first. Still, there's no denying that this got on Tom's nerves after a while, well after multiple interruptions to his leadership talk.

It was usually Paul who shouted 'Line' or 'Two Fat Bastards to go' when he was close. Tom tolerated it to a point but then would yell back something intended to call a halt to the banter that wouldn't have been out of place on the Bingo card itself.

"Paul! Enough man! Put it in the parking lot until later!"

He successfully silenced the room but, as soon as Tom's back was turned, Paul would mouth 'Fuckin' parking lot' at me, whilst I shrugged my shoulders and he shook his head.

Another example of our collective professionalism was when Liz had gone missing from the meeting for a while. When she walked back in, the senior management team were in the middle of a corporate debate on anal sex, as you would expect in a leadership meeting. She flounced back into the room and declared, with absolute certainty, that 'the marmite motorway should be a one-way street' followed by 'no dirty bastard will be getting his brown wings by tinkering with my precious starfish'. It was both amazing and refreshing to witness someone speaking on a matter with such conviction and unprepared - a masterclass. And, in a senior management meeting too.

Safe to say, I was getting to know everyone much better. Matt couldn't quite believe the stories

I'd come home with; tales about what had happened that day or what certain colleagues had said. He was most amused and wanted to know more about everyone before he met them at the next social event when the company invited spouses and partners. I prepared him by giving daily recaps.

There was Liz in Supply Chain with her impressively ample bosom; Liz was super loud in all she did but extremely funny and hugely committed to the job and her customers. Pricetown Store Managers, men or women, who appreciated the wit of outrageous sexual linguists loved her. For the remainder, Liz knew when to tone it down.

Lindsey in accounts was a prickly character but practically climaxed over spreadsheets. If the numbers didn't drive the decision, she didn't know how to process the information. For example, when we were discussing whether or not to grant paid bereavement to someone upon losing a close relative, her starting point was 'if it isn't in the budget, or written in stone, then we shouldn't even be thinking about it'.

I would lead the charge in favour of looking after people in their hour of need and she would say I was too soft. We had the odd heated exchange when I had to continuously remind her not to confuse soft with compassionate and humane. We had a lot of employees who were related to and living in the local area. Reputation mattered. She wasn't a bad person, just super stiff. In the main, she was so prim and proper that Paul Tetley christened her 'Chanel Knickers'. She used to say things like, 'I'm going have to slap some wrists if you don't have the correct receipts for your expenses'. People were tempted to reply in an equally squeaky tone, 'I'm going to have to punch you in the face if you do.'

Then there was Tom, MD, perpetually flustered, prone to barking orders at those around him. Not in a horrible way, just in an abrupt, middle-aged '70s kind of way. As previously mentioned, one of his favourite soundbites had become, 'Gemma, you're in charge of morale.' This phrase came right after he had casually made an announcement such as, 'We're closing down five departments over the next month; get it done and keep people smiling. We can't miss a single delivery'. Luckily, I love a challenge.

I must not forget Paul Tetley, a constant source of amusement, horror and suspense. The one-man walking employment tribunal who would wipe the floor with you if you displayed any form of incompetence or made a mistake. However, in the next breath, he would get his team to valet your car every week and fill it with fuel. I couldn't help liking him on a personal level, he did, strangely enough, look after me and he was amusing. That said, I once told him straight that, whilst he was very funny, he was going to get the business in trouble. And when he did, he'd be on his own in court. Sadly, he was 'all out of fucks' concerning that particular piece of advice.

"Aye, alright, whatever you say sweet cheeks! It'll be reet," he assured me in true PT style.

My closest HR colleague, both geographically and later in terms of friendship, was Dawn. She was highly experienced in the HR role. She was a straight-talking, no-nonsense, salt of the earth Oldham lass with the work rate of one of Marvel's Avengers. She showed me the ropes, mentored me and was like a protective 'big sister' at work. She put her arm around me when I needed support; turned it into a headlock when something needed doing differently or quickly - a perfect combination! I shadowed Dawn more than anyone else in the early years, due to the position of our sites. I was learning lots and could see the opportunities for further development ahead of me.

Between Jan, Dawn, the national HR team and myself, we achieved a great deal and it was great being part of a team that was known for delivering over and above expectations. Maybe not quite the Charlie's Angels of HR (I wouldn't want to be immodest) but some of the issues we resolved would have troubled LA's finest all-female crime-fighting team. Maybe Paul Tetley could have filled the shoes of Charlie, albeit a much more contentious, outrageous one.

There was more than one occasion when things were awkward, thanks to Paul's repartee. I gained experience and after an HR re-shuffle, I was promoted to look after the entire site as well as a sister-site down the road. Dawn could look after the depots in South Yorkshire as she had recently married and relocated to that neck of the woods. We were still in touch but didn't see each other all the time. It was handy because my new responsibilities included managing payroll for both sites and the team that processed it - my first taste of line management. Luckily, Dawn was on top of things and had run a tight ship. However, as soon as she had left, the payroll team saw an opportunity to cast their web of influence into areas they shouldn't, frequently pushing the boundaries.

The payroll department comprised of a rich, all-female, tapestry of experience who were all in their early fifties. Not that this should count for anything, but conversations would often be in full flow along the following lines, 'I'm sorry, love, I'll be with you in a minute when I've opened these windows and shoved a cold compress down my top.'

'I didn't get a wink of sleep last night, Sandra. I was perspiring slightly with my symptoms and Billy asked me to go in the spare room coz the bed sheets were soaked! I was hoping for some sympathy, but he said that I was sweating like a boar with a raw bollock and I had to shift myself!'

'I can't understand why I keep putting weight on. I know my body is going through some natural changes, but I can't seem to keep the weight off anymore. Éclair anyone?'

'I'm just off to the Spar for some 'Always Ultra'.

I need night-time specials with wings and a two-way dry weave top sheet these days. I keep getting caught short with my monthlies. Anybody want a Twix whilst I'm there?'

A few people, such as Paul, managed to get away with a level of banter that others couldn't. It was usually after they'd offended one of his drivers, or they hadn't paid them properly and had given them short shrift. He would ring up and, after being ignored a few times or if his request had not been dealt with, he would revert to type. He'd say things like 'Morning! I have an important question that will require your expert professional opinions. What is the difference between you lot and a pit bull? Lipstick!' Occasionally one of them would cackle a response along the lines of, 'All our problems start with 'men' Paul - *men*opause, *men*tal breakdowns and *men*struation.' This was usually enough to make him wince and walk out of the office or put the phone down.

Each of them had been with the business, in various guises, since Adam was a lad. There was nothing that they thought they didn't know. They showed empathy for those who they liked and thinly veiled contempt for those they didn't. If they liked you, they might pay you properly. If they got your pay wrong and they liked you, they would correct the error straight away and send the correct money to the bank. If they liked you and had done nothing wrong from a process perspective, but you happened to be a bit skint that week, they might seek authorisation for a loan to tide you over. However, if they got your pay wrong and *didn't* like you, you were screwed. They would tell you, in no uncertain terms, that you'd have to wait until the next payday, even if this meant you couldn't feed your children. The balance of power was wrong. Standard processes were all too often at the mercy of the subjective opinion of Sharon Zallinski, the Payroll Manager.

Let's just say that Sharon and I didn't see eye to eye. Looking back, I'd heard Dawn mention 'the formidable Zallinski' but I didn't realise the full picture until I met her. She was not one to mince her words; Sharon's opening gambit in her first meeting with me as her new line manager comprised of, 'So, the thing is, we loved Dawn. Such an amazing woman to work for. We don't know you yet and don't want to get to know you. We don't like or trust Jan because she's never here. So, if it's ok with you, I'd like you just to let us carry on doing our thing. You and Jan do yours and we can all just leave each other to it. There's no real need to interact or socialise with each other. You can trust us to get on with it, no questions asked. Agreed?'

A true master of passive aggression, she said all of this with a smile on her face. Although momentarily lost for words, I managed a calm yet assertive, 'No, I'm afraid I can't agree to that Sharon'. I followed this with a lengthy explanation about how vital local communication was, especially given the widespread nature of our organisational structure. How our sites were tiny cogs in a big wheel, so, unless we operated as a close-knit team, further success would be jeopardised. I explained that I thought daily catch up meetings would be a good idea and would give this more thought before we introduced them.

Crunch time came when I stated that I would be happy to pass her reservations on to Jan and Tom if she wanted to discuss further the organisational structure. Unsurprisingly, she politely declined. However, I was duty-bound to tell Jan. She was livid, more out of defence of me than anything. She felt that she had given the team plenty of freedom and autonomy when conducting their work. She was, of course, aware of the frosty atmosphere, but had been sure this would thaw over time, given a chance. This is what got on Jan's nerves the most - the fact that we hadn't been given an opportunity. The tipping point came when Jan accidentally flouted Sharon's kitchenette policy. Yes, you read that correctly. Like all 'mini-overlords' who are dangerous when given an ounce of responsibility, Sharon had a kitchenette policy for all users of the brewing up and associated fridge area in the offices.

Sharon's rules included:

- Only two people at a time are allowed in the kitchenette for reasons of hygiene. *(More on this later!)*.

- Any out-of-date unused food will be checked daily and thrown out *(most people suspected that Sharon gave herself the role of food police so that she could take any leftovers home for her tea without suspicion. Save her cooking for the night).*

- Theft of food would be punishable by death *(well not really but almost. The case of the missing mint sauce was a conundrum, despite the fact that Sharon had been spotted with a conspicuous green stain down her mustard yellow C&A blouse).*

- You had to leave the kitchenette as you would expect to find it *(even if you weren't the one who had made a mackerel curry for lunch that had simultaneously exploded in the microwave, crusting it over in a matter of seconds. Tough luck - you were expected to clean it up should you find it and then, clean it again after you'd warmed up your innocuous bowl of soup).*

- Most importantly of all, you were not, under any circumstances, allowed to fill the kettle past level four, which was a good centimetre off the 'max' mark. *(This was because it would overflow when it came to boiling point. To help any unwitting users, Sharon had painted a line in Tippex at the right point on the kettle and left helpful 'post-it' notes on all jars and boxes of tea, coffee and 'cuppa soups' in the area. Most people who worked on-site full time, instinctively knew to follow this rule because it was ingrained - like riding a bike or writing your name. For less frequent visitors to the site, the message was less clear. People such as Jan didn't know the rules and brought their own teabags in and so hadn't needed to access anything other than hot water in the kitchen.)*

One fateful morning, Jan was hurriedly making a brew and overfilled the kettle. I'm sure that Sharon's kettle-level spidey senses were tingling, even at this point. Jan filled it up, popped out of the kitchenette whilst it boiled, spoke to a few people working in the vicinity and went back in to make her brew. She noticed a small amount of water on the worktop and dutifully mopped it up, collected her cuppa and went back to her desk.

Unfortunately, Jan hadn't noticed it dripping into the drawer where all the cutlery, napkins and other utensils were kept. Or, that it had seeped onto the floor and was slowly, but surely, creeping towards the kitchenette entrance and doorway.

When, twenty minutes later, Sharon rocked up to make her morning coffee with just the *right* amount of water and had skidded across the kitchenette into the arms of a very bemused Tony Slater, she was not pleased. His hair was the colour of burnt orange that day (in case you were wondering) with a natural silver goatee beard to match (or maybe not). Tony, on the other hand, for a moment, thought his luck was in.

Sharon launched a full, Agatha Christie-style, investigation into who could be responsible for such reckless behaviour. With her sleuth-like skills of elimination, she narrowed it down to Jan. Of course, she didn't take the most common-sense orientated route – that of having a quiet word with Jan - a very reasonable woman who would have understood completely. Sharon decided that such an epic scale deviation from the kitchen rules was deserving of more severe action, so she leapfrogged Jan and me straight to Tom. He had nothing better to do than deal with 'Kettlegate'. I rushed down to his office after receiving the inevitable call, 'Gemma. You better get down here. It's all kicking off!'

Thinking that I was about to have to deal with some kind of dispute with the union, I was surprised to find Sharon at the desk in tears. Not the bitter tears of a woman who had just pirouetted into Tony, (which would be enough to reduce most normal, sane women to tears) but angry tears because Jan had not followed her precious policy.

Crying middle-aged women were not Tom's strong point. I quickly realised this as he shot panicked looks my way in between tentative pats on Sharon's back, all the time saying 'there, there' in semi-soothing tones. At that moment, I assured Tom that I would sort it.

Whisking Sharon off to my office, I calmed her down, made her a brew (from a kettle filled just to the right level) called maintenance and asked if the budget would stretch to a hot water boiler and dispenser for the kitchenette. As luck would have it, it would. In the meantime, we would borrow a kettle from the canteen. I knew that moments like these satisfied the four years at uni and a post-graduate diploma in all things HR. Joking aside, I came to appreciate that conflict resolution, on the seemingly smallest level, was a crucial part of keeping the Harfield wheels turning. We all have our foibles and quirks. Being listened to sensitively is always an essential part of the process and the key to moving forward.

Once things had calmed down and the moment was right, I suggested to Sharon that this could and should have been avoided, or at least managed with more composure than it had been. I was cool but calm and not unkind. I had hoped for the same reaction from Sharon.

"But Jan didn't follow my rules and didn't observe the line on the kettle drawn in brilliant white!" she raged.

"Sharon, I know your rules are well intended, but Jan is an occasional visitor to the site and she didn't know that they existed. You or I - or both of us - should have given her the 'heads up' about the kettle, but we didn't. Don't take it personally - things like this happen all the time, not on purpose or out of bad intentions - they just happen. In HR, we have to take the drama out of heated situations like this, be the measured ones, not make things worse. So, I'm asking you to take it in your stride and not get stressed about it. Also, if anything happens in the future that you're upset about, you need to come to me first, give me the chance to deal with it. Going to Tom about a kettle is arguably over the top when he has a national carrot famine to deal with and serious conversations with suppliers. This concern was not something he should even be aware of." I had hoped she would understand.

"Yes, ok, I suppose I understand," said Sharon, as she pottered out of my office, eyes dried and headed back to her own.

So, all was well, apart from Jan who thought that the whole thing was absurd. She wanted to tell Sharon to 'shove her kitchenette policy up her arse'. She even threatened to transfer her to the Wigan site (a fate no one should be threatened with). I implored her to leave Sharon and the team to me, which she did. We were making progress overall. She went further and made a point of speaking with Sharon calmly and sweetly, ensuring that the air had been cleared. It was a masterclass in killing someone with kindness but, underneath it all, Jan remained determined that things had to change.

With immediate effect, Jan insisted that the payroll team should start producing reports detailing time spent actively processing payroll, sick pay, pay discrepancies and corrective actions taken. Report writing was something entirely new for them. To be fair, a lot of the other sites were already producing this information. So, it wasn't entirely out of the blue or a knee jerk reaction to what Sharon had said. I knew I would be the one who had to make the request to soften the blow. I noted that it was to bring us in line with other sites. It offered an excellent opportunity to showcase our phenomenal work rate and departmental output.

At first, Sharon was dubious. She said it felt like 'Big Brother' was watching, which of course it was, to a point. I said it was not dissimilar to the information I had to take to management meetings each week, just a distinct set of data. This process was the way of the world in HR, across many businesses.

This was true. The profession was transitioning from the old days of 'Personnel' (with connotations of paying people cash in brown envelopes and offering endless amounts of tea and sympathy) to 'Human Resources'. The new regime was more business-like and professional, thus earning a place at the board room table. However, Sharon didn't care two fat frogs about the theory. Or indeed articles produced by our industry body, the Chartered Institute of Personnel and Development (CIPD), of which the entire HR team were members.

We all had to pass the exams to be able to use the letters after our name. Qualifications carried a particular kudos, but there was no substitute for experience. Times were changing. HR was expected to be more strategic; taking a business-partnering approach to work, firmly representing the business before the people. It was a step-change that not everybody liked but done well, a balance could still be found and put into effect.

Nonetheless, changes were introduced and, after a couple of months at the bottom of the league table across all sites, we started to rise through the charts. Jan asked probing questions, making it clear that we needed to see improvements. I worked hard in the background to try and increase our scores. It was very gratifying to see that a tweak here and a change there would work. We involved the team in everything that we did and their ideas impacted results for the better. I don't believe that league tables should necessarily drive good service, real work and delivering results on time, but it introduced a sense of accountability. This safety-net had previously been missing and - dare I say it - offered a sense of professional pride and an improved reputation.

I'm pleased to say that Sharon and I managed to forge a polite, professional relationship over time. I only wish I could say that Paul Tetley had managed to do the same, but alas, no. His banter with the team may have been well-received but, where Sharon Zalinski was concerned, his acid tongue knew no bounds. He didn't like her. Nothing I could say about working relationships could change that. I begged him to be at least professional. He grudgingly agreed to do so but, in practice, he carried on regardless.

One sunny afternoon, after visiting the department in person, he asked me for a word in my office. Of course, this could be about anything, considering the roulette wheel that was Paul's mouth.

"How the fuck can you stand it?" he asked.

"Stand what?" I asked, not knowing what he meant.

"That stench when you walk into payroll. I shit you not, that woman smells like a horse blanket. You take your life into your own hands when you walk in there on a warm afternoon."

"That's a bit strong!" I replied, knowing full well who and what he meant.

"Strong?! I'll tell you what's fuckin' strong. Sharon's body-odour smacks you right in the mush when you walk in. I know the window latch is a bit sticky in there and 'comb-over boy' is too tight to stick his hand in his pocket and pay for air-con. But someone needs to tell her that it's not ok to slip off her shoes and walk round in tights when it's nearly thirty degrees outside and your trotters smell of horse shite! I wouldn't mind, but she wears fifty denier, even in June. It smells like vinegar in there on a good day. I don't know how the rest of them cope with it in that office. She stinks and you need to say something to her because I for one, would rather lick my arsehole than go in there without a mask and full body armour, which cannot be right."

'Oh God', I thought to myself, knowing that he was right. I also knew that, at some point, I'd have to have one of the most awkward and sensitive conversations that you could have with anyone at work, just as we were getting along so well.

I often had to work in the payroll department to oversee the payroll activity, giving direction or sign off on certain payments and benefits, such as sick pay. When we had HR team meetings, they would be in their office, as it was bigger than mine, accommodating around six people. It was a busy department, with a steady stream of people coming with payroll queries and the phone ringing non-stop. Sometimes, when the phone rang and we were in the middle of something, we'd hit the speaker button so that the caller was speaking to the room. This arrangement was all very good when normal people called, but when it was Paul Tetley, you might be greeted with, 'Now then, is the Toby Jug there?' (a Paul Tetley nod to Sharon's weight and body shape).

'Can I speak to the bag of shit or is she tied up?' (Sharon, again).

'Is Stinky Winky in today or what?' (again, Sharon).

'Where's the wet dog?' (guess who?)

'Four-cheese sauce feet, please?' (you've got it!).

'Champion the fucking Wonder Horse please, or if not, his blanket will do,' was his particular favourite. Sometimes he'd just neigh down the phone like one of our equine friends.

Most of the time it seemed to go over Sharon's head. Her ignorance was our bliss (sheer relief that she hadn't twigged). I thank my lucky stars to this very day that she had never heard enough to complain and that the rest of the team went into super polite and professional 'help' mode to assist glossing over things by frantically picking up their handset. I think they were trying to save their own blushes as much as Sharon's.

The day came when the matter needed confronting - time to seize my moment. After a couple of months of being Sharon's line manager and comments from more than one of my management colleagues about the aroma in the office, I approached the conversation with some trepidation.

By now, we were getting along on a professional level, but we hardly had a relationship built on the most solid foundation. A conversation about 'l'odeur corporelle' wasn't going to help improve matters. I asked Jan and Dawn (who I was still in touch with) for guidance on how to manage the conversation. They had known Sharon far longer than I had and must have known about the problem in question. I thought that they would have the right words or be able to tell me that it had already been dealt with. Maybe my conversation with her would act as a gentle reminder of what had been said before. Fortifying words of encouragement did indeed come from them in the form of, 'Crack on, it's good for your personal development'. Dawn admitted that she'd known for years about the odour problem and had actively avoided having any kind of conversation about it with Sharon. Jan was more sympathetic, but it was clear that I needed to 'woman up' and have the conversation. I knew they were right, but it was hardly the script for success that I was relishing.

The time arrived for the big chat. I made Sharon a cuppa from the new hot water dispenser (it was the least I could do) and initially we passed pleasantries about how things were going in general. She seemed fine, but all of that was about to change.

"Whilst I have you, I've been wondering if everything is ok with you, health-wise?"

"Yes, why?"

"Well, it's a very sensitive topic to have to speak to someone about, but I hope you can understand that what I'm about to say is coming from a good place and an angle of wanting to help."

"Go on," said Sharon, nervously.

"Well, cutting straight to the chase, I've had some reports that you might have a body odour or cleanliness problem, which is a difficult thing to hear. I'm not judging at all, but I wondered if there might be any medical or health issues that could be underlying?"

"What?" cried Sharon indignantly. "Who from? Tell me their names!" she demanded.

"Names don't matter and you know I can't tell you who, but I have to say that I've noticed it myself and I wanted to speak with you about it, one to one. It's only fair that you know. Please don't think anyone is being unkind here, but I do feel that you should be aware of what's being said because I

71

would want to know if it was me. If there's anything you want to tell me or anything I can do to help, I will."

"I'll have you know I have a bath every Sunday and sometimes midweek without fail!" said Sharon indignantly. 'That often?' I thought to myself. Sharon was now purple with rage and about to blow a horsey gasket, but clearly, she was deeply embarrassed about the whole thing.

"Well, maybe you could have them more regularly, or perhaps take a shower in between. Are you ok using shower gel, washing powder and deodorants? I know some people can be sensitive to them."

"Well, deodorants make me itch. I do wash my clothes, but I haven't got anywhere to dry them, so I just fold them up wet and leave them to dry," Sharon said. That would explain the whiff of wet dog then!

"Ok, well why don't we help by getting you a clothes airer and perhaps you could speak with Occupational Health about deodorant for sensitive skin that might work for you? You're not alone; you know this happens to a lot of people." I offered, as sympathetically as possible.

"Yes, ok, I suppose so," said Sharon.

"I can speak with Occ Health and I'll think about bathing more often. I'm surprised my husband hasn't mentioned it, but we both share the same bath water once a week, so maybe we don't notice each other?" she offered.

I didn't want to dwell on that image. I knew Sam; he worked on the shop floor. Knowing also that he and Sharon had two grown-up sons living at home, I didn't want to delve into just how far that weekly bathwater went.

"Ok, I'm glad we've had this chat. Please be assured that it will remain confidential and you can talk to me at any time about this and it will stay between us." I swiftly concluded.

"Yes, ok. I suppose I'm glad you've told me and I will speak to Occ Health and make those changes," said Sharon, committedly.

We now had an understanding and that was ok with me. I made a mental note to speak with Paul about his inappropriate telephone greetings and from then on, things were okay with the team and me. I even trained a couple of them to become HR Officers and shadow me in areas they'd not previously experienced. One went on to become regional HR Director for Pricetown, which was great for her. Overall, the team learned to embrace the data-driven decision making that we introduced regarding payroll. It made processes more efficient and life easier overall. I'm not sure they ever grew to love Jan and me, but they did respect our way of doing things. They didn't come to me with any more outrageous demands regarding how we should communicate with each other or brew up. Job done.

You'll be pleased to know that Sharon began to shower more regularly, found a deodorant and shower gel range that didn't make her itch and used the clotheshorse we bought to hang her clothes on to dry. Sharon herself was much happier and the quality of the air much-improved.

That said, when my boyfriend, Matt, came along to the summer party later that year. Sharon put his tie around her head whilst dancing with some ferocity to 'Man, I feel like a woman', he politely said she could keep it when she tried to give the tie back at the end of the night, dripping in perspiration.

Ah well, one step at a time, I guess!

Chapter 5

Good HR Support is Hard to Find

As my role evolved along with the business, it became clear that the company wanted me in more meetings. On occasions, I had to leave my busy day-to-day HR role. Sometimes, the payroll team could help out, but there were certain times in the week when they couldn't, as they needed to be fully focused on their payroll duties.

It became busy enough to warrant an extra pair of hands. Tracey arrived to offer admin support. With it being the 90's, all our records were still on paper, stored in eight-foot filing cabinets. Tracey's remit was to help sort the filing system, keep on top of the admin and answer the phone when I wasn't there. Her remit was most definitely not to get rat-arsed on a lunchtime or have her wicked way with one of the FLT drivers from Goods-In. However, she did have the decency to scuttle off into the IT server room. This room, apparently, offered them warmth and shelter on bitterly cold winter days. Sadly, this incident was compounded by Tracey regularly being found slumped at the bottom of the filing cabinet surrounded by miniatures and a hip flask. The 'help' she offered and her employment with the business, was short-lived. We offered to assist her in getting on track and looked into numerous ways in which we could provide support, but none stuck.

The reliability just wasn't there.

"To be honest love…" hiccupped Tracey as I explained that things weren't working out. "I do love having a bevvy at lunchtime and I'd probably do it again. I can't help myself. I only shagged Dean in the IT room coz he said he had a hip flask."

So, Tracey understood how things had to be, but I always regretted that we couldn't help her turn things around. She was quite helpful, when sober and pleasant when conscious. Tracey had fallen victim to her addiction, which impacted on every other aspect of her life. I told her that the door was always open if she could get herself clean and she thanked me for at least trying to help.

We were back to square one. However, more help was to come in the form of Sandra, already a receptionist extraordinaire. Everybody loved Sandra. She was friendly, professional and super-efficient. Randomly, Tom had recently asked me to manage reception (along with the canteen and security, naturally), so I was delighted when Sandra expressed an interest in learning the ropes of HR. She seemed on the ball, up for it and keen to get started, but, to allow it to happen, we needed to find cover for Sandra on reception.

Like all good employers, we advertised the vacancy internally and eagerly awaited the applications. The only direction I received from Tom was, 'Don't pick a numpty'. Jan was happy for me to crack on and soon the time for interviews arrived. I asked Sandra to make the decision with me, as she knew the role inside out. However, halfway through the second interview, Tony Slater knocked on the door (he was blonde that day by the way - platinum) and said, "Sorry to interrupt, but Denise Smith has just told us she's pregnant and she's worried about all the lifting she has to do. She's scared we might fire her. She's locked herself in the toilet and is refusing to come out. Can you have a word?" he asked. I gave my apologies to Sandra and the candidate and off I went.

I'm not sure just how long I was gone. I had to find Denise, convince her to come out of the loo and reassure her that we could accommodate her on light duties. However, it was enough time to miss most of the interviews. I'd only met candidate number one. Sandra had whizzed through the other sessions as she'd never done it before and was rather nervous. I asked her if she thought she had found anyone; although the particular candidate had been nervous herself and had not said much, she was the only candidate who had changed out of her warehouse PPE and dressed for the role. I asked Sandra if she'd managed to get hold of Tony or John to ask about the candidate's work record. Tony had confirmed that she was hard-working but quiet. 'Good enough.' Julie O'Grady would start with a trial period the following morning.

Julie was in bright and early and ready to go. She was even in before Sandra and that was saying something. I know that Sandra spent the first half of the morning showing her the ropes, opening the post and listening in on calls so that Julie could come to terms with the vast switchboard, which resembled something from NASA. I popped down to ask how it was going. Sandra reported that Julie was quiet but listening well. We agreed that the training should continue, but we should let Julie greet the next visitor and answer a couple of calls. Big mistake. Always do your homework during any recruitment process.

Julie had expressed extreme nervousness to Sandra about taking calls. She said she could get her head around most of the tasks she'd been shown so far but, without being specific, phones worried her. Doing her best to assure Julie that everything would be ok and that she would jump in if needed, the ladies agreed that Julie would answer the next call that came in. It happened to be from one of the Pricetown stores near Runcorn. The manager was looking for Liz but couldn't get hold of her. He was usually a jovial chap but was a bit stressed this particular day as a pallet of yoghurt and a cage of milk hadn't been delivered as expected.

"If you could just track her down for me love or put me through to wherever she is, that would be great," said the store manager innocently.

Julie became flustered and put him through to three different departments. As he came back on the phone, he was astonished to hear her shouting "shit… fuck…. wank stain…"

"Beg your pardon, love?" he gently inquired.

Sandra quickly stepped in. Offered apologies and tracked down the right department for the unsuspecting customer. Before Sandra could ask Julie what she was thinking, in walked a visitor through the reception doors. It happened to be Tom's boss, Business Unit Director, George Pickwick.

"Good morning!" he bellowed. "George Pickwick to see Tom Pringle. I don't believe I've seen you before honey-pot. My my, aren't you a pretty one?" he said to Julie as he perched on the desk

"Fuck you… Arsehole… Dickhead… Shit moustache…" replied Julie, in quick succession. The poor chap quickly jumped up as Sandra escorted him to the sofas, offering profuse apologies for Julie's misdemeanours as calmly as she could.

"I'm so sorry, we're just in her first morning of training and it must have all got a bit much for her. The pressure is quite intense in here sometimes, but you take a nice comfy seat. I'll bring you a coffee and let Tom know that you're here," offered Sandra apologetically.

She turned to face Julie who had scuttled off into the back office, mortified. "What were you thinking?" asked Sandra. "Is everything ok?"

Sniffling loudly, Julie said, "I'm so sorry about that, I suppose I should have told you that I have - fuck… shit… bollocks… bitch… Tourette's

Syndrome. I wanted this opportunity to work out, but the pressure on the phones and then when George... wanker... arse badger... jizz cock... walked in. I kind of lost control. It's worse when I'm under pressure. I'm so sorry!"

"It's ok; it's not your fault," offered Sandra. "But you might have mentioned it in the interview before we put you in front of house."

"I know," sniffed Julie. "I am so sorry."

"Did Tony know about this, as your line manager?" asked Sandra.

"Yes. Dickhead... thundercunt... bell end... shag master... wig. Sorry. Yes, he did. I don't try and hide it, but I do keep my head down and get on with the job usually. John is very supportive, but if Tony's on shift... cock... wank stain... shit hair... then he'll sometimes take the mick, but he'll let me get on with it. Most people are understanding, but it's hard sometimes."

"Ok," said Sandra, "why don't we make you a cuppa and go and have a chat with Gemma?"

"Ok. Will she understand?" worried Julie.

"Yes, Gemma will, for sure." Sandra comforted.

So, up they popped and relayed the story. It turns out that Julie was the sister-in-law of Alex, the union rep, so he accompanied her in the meeting for support. I was sympathetic to Julie's situation and, even though I knew I was in for a kickin' from Tom and possibly Jan for letting this happen on the front desk, I didn't want her to feel worse than she already did.

We had a good chat about her condition, which had manifested itself out of nowhere in her early forties. Her father had suffered from the same affliction, so she had a feeling that it was hereditary, but there was no medical proof of that. Julie had always done her best to live with it, keeping her head down at work and avoiding social interaction. She was embarrassed by the affliction. She confirmed that the symptoms were worse when she was anxious or feeling self-conscious. Tracey knew she should have told us when applying for the reception role, but she wanted to give it her best shot and was afraid that the outcome would have been pre-judged if she'd said anything. She might have had a good point!

We had a long chat and I was as sympathetic and supportive as I could have been. I was keen to understand what the business could do to help Tracey and wanted her to know that the door was always open if she ever wanted to chat. I liked Julie. She was a grafter, tried to give herself better opportunities and wasn't afraid to go for it. I admired that. Alex was very supportive of her and keen that everyone should move on quickly from this and return to normal. Just before the meeting ended, I asked Julie again if there was anything we could do to help more at work.

"Well, there is one thing you could do, maybe," said Julie. Keen to know the answer, I asked her to tell us. "Well, if I could get a job in admin on days it would help with the tiredness levels. Working nights gets to you after a while. Plus, I'd be away from Tony Slater tosser... knob cheese... gobshite... bollock face. Sorry. It's just that most people I work with are great and take the piss in a light-hearted way. Most of them went to school with me, so I'm used to them, but Tony arse wipe... todger... chode... smeghead. He's nasty with it sometimes and he doesn't know me well enough to take the piss in the same way as the others."

What an education in new cuss words! How was it with Tourette's, that unsavoury words spring forth to the mouth? Perfectly reasonable, professional, hard-working family people verbalising profanities that they would never usually use. I couldn't help smiling at Julie's request. I think Alex, Sandra and Julie knew that I wanted to help. I assured them that I would make some enquiries and see what we could do.

At the end of the meeting, Alex thanked me for being so understanding. I told them that this was an end to the matter but encouraged Julie that she should be open about having Tourette's. Alex was keen to know that no further action would be taken against Julie. I assured him there wouldn't be - I would take one for this particular team. Sandra looked relieved at this outcome.

"I think we need to be grateful that Gemma is the manager in charge of reception here, Julie," said

Alex as they stood up to leave the room. "Other managers wouldn't have been so understanding."

"Yes," said Julie. "I can't thank you enough and I am sorry for any trouble I've caused. I do appreciate your support. From the bottom of my heart I just want to say Fuck You Gemma, Fuck You." Wonderful! I didn't bother correcting her as I *think* I knew what she meant. As Alex and Julie left the room. Sandra stayed back for a minute and was uber-apologetic. "I'm so sorry, I had no idea. I should have checked - been more thorough."

"You and me both." I smiled at her. "Don't worry, these things happen. Maybe we could see some of the other candidates again to see if we think they could give reception training a shot. I'd still like you to train in HR if you're up for it - I think you'd be great." Grateful for that conclusion, Sandra said she'd love to still work in the department. She went back to reception, addressed the waiting visitors and took the switchboard off 'night mode' to continue her day job. I scampered down the corridor to Tom's office to face the inevitable music.

As I walked in, Jan was already sitting there. Gulp. I hadn't realised she was visiting today and she must have gone straight to see Tom when she arrived on site. Double-whammy-bollocking was coming right up, or so I thought. I launched straight into my apologies, taking the blame, explaining that I should have checked more thoroughly and not taken Tony's word for it without digging deeper. I said it was down to me and no one else. I knew I should have conducted more checks and possibly spoken with Dawn about Julie's history, but I hadn't. What I hadn't noticed initially was that Tom and Jan were smirking, having been giggling with each other for the last few minutes. Thankfully, they saw the funny side. Tom even said "The best thing is that Julie was right about George. He does have a shit moustache and should have shaved it off ten years ago. He's always getting peas stuck and bits of custard drying off in it. He's also a bit of a wannabe womaniser and might think twice before flirting with the workforce now he's had a reality check." Phew. I'd got away with it thankfully. We had a good laugh together behind closed doors when I related Julie's parting comments to me. Priceless.

Lesson learned, check, double-check and check again when hiring people, internally or externally. At the very least it will potentially save you time and possible embarrassment in the long run.

Chapter 6

There's Nowt as Queer as Folk

Most people I met at Harfield Distribution were as sound as a pound. Some simply wanted to come to work, get the job done and go home with no more responsibility than that. That was fine with me - we need good foot soldiers in every walk of life. Not everyone can be, or indeed wants to be a Galactico. Good job too.

I was starting to understand people and their circumstances much more than I had, matching their aspirations and ambitions with the needs of the business. We introduced appraisals -actually quite good ones! Not too time consuming - thirty minutes per employee every quarter. This initiative was better than some horrendous annual process that took hours to prepare and was then put into a drawer for another twelve months. Now, managers could identify skill gaps and offer opportunities for those who wanted to work in other departments. We introduced training matrices for each role so that people could be signed off as competent in a specific position before moving on. For new starters, this was helpful, as they knew what was expected of them in practical terms. It also meant that those who wanted to move on and become competent in other areas could do so and those who didn't weren't forced in that direction. Eventually, the broader your skill set, the more you earned. This situation seemed fair and the union agreed.

Pretty soon we had a clear, transparent career path mapped out across the shop floor, with some managers better at implementing it than others. The beauty of it was that the people drove the success of the system - if they were forced to work in a department they didn't like, they soon made it known. If we weren't providing the opportunity for progression that people craved, they complained and we rectified it. Simple.

I was no stranger to conversations along the lines of, 'Listen, love, I need to get myself upskilled. More skills mean more money. I've promised the wife a bangin' trip to Bridlington next summer, so if you could have a word and speed it all up, I'd be very grateful. I'm sick of the sight of milk and cheese now. I've been on that aisle so long that I've been robbed of the simple pleasures of Welsh Rarebit and a milky Horlicks. Gone. Finito. End of. If you could get me into the freezer pronto, me and the wife would be very happy.'

Alternatively, 'Can you tell Tony and John to stop making me work in fruit. I have no desire to leave Müller yoghurts and work in an area that stocks naturally occurring sugars. I don't want to earn any more money and I have an unconfirmed allergy to kumquats.'

You can't please all of the people all of the time and no matter what systems and opportunities you have created, you can't legislate for some people's actions or their behaviours.

The HR role was as meaty and varied as I had hoped it would be. On the downside, I was also getting to know that theft was par for the course at Harfield. Bear in mind that we distributed to Pricetown and stored absolutely everything in our warehouse that you would see in a Pricetown store (other than cigarettes and alcohol, but that's a whole different story).

Across the warehouses, we had everything from clothing and SIM cards to olives and salami. Sometimes the temptations proved to be too great for people to keep at bay. Theft was so prevalent at one stage that we ran out of warehouse managers and supervisors to conduct the disciplinaries. Often managers from other departments had to be brought in to show segregation between the investigation and disciplinary processes. Tom told me we needed to do something about it as Harfield had to foot the bill for any missing stock. We had to up the ante to reduce the number of people who were stealing.

We introduced tighter security and installed CCTV cameras across the warehouses. We started to catch more people in the act, although it never quite felt like a victory to me. One of the first employees to get caught under this new regime was Simon Glenn. Once, he managed to leave work wearing seven pairs of Levis. He was a dodgy character who had, for some time, been suspected of theft. Now he'd been caught on camera towards the end of an early shift. He was looking a tad shady - prancing about on the spot and lunging in the shadows of the warehouse, measuring himself up for a perfect fit. However, his 'Michelin Man' gait gave him away as he shuffled along to his car. He was duly busted by security.

My primary advice for Simon and indeed anyone wishing to steal clothing, was not to be greedy, especially if you're going to wear the hot goods during your getaway. The one thing you won't pull off is the transformation from a slimly built, regular guy who walks normally one minute, to a rather rotund looking fat Santa lumbering along like John Wayne. People - and more specifically, security - will notice!

Another employee, let's call him Jerry - because that was his name - was caught with two (of what *would* have been Pricetown's Finest) fillet steaks strapped to his chest. His excuse when caught was, 'But I'm going to transition soon. I've got the operation booked in and I need to get used to what it feels like to have tits. The more practice I get, the better.' Give me strength I cried, inwardly.

Outwardly Jason, his union rep, implored us to look favourably on this case. It was starting to be a topical subject attracting increased media interest in the trans world and the processes that people went through physically, hormonally and mentally.

Unfortunately, during the subsequent disciplinary

meeting, there was nothing inward or newsworthy about Paul Tetley's thoughts. Despite my best efforts to encourage him not to pre-judge anything from the investigation notes and to keep an open mind, he started the meeting in his most incredulous tone with, 'You're telling me that you're fuckin' transitioning? You want tits? Actual tits? I'll tell you all you need to know about tits lad. You are possibly the biggest tit I have ever met. You are such a massive tit for stealing from the place that pays your wages that I'm surprised you can see your own fuckin' shoes. For certain, you are as much use as tits on Grandma so get your stuff and piss off out of it. You're sacked.' I remember relating this story to Dawn and she confirmed that Jerry had tried the same infraction with some pink grapefruits a few months earlier, but no hard evidence could be found.

I should have been used to it by now, but I was still slightly open-mouthed at this one. My meeting notes were sparse, but I remembered to offer Jerry the right to appeal. This offer hadn't been high on Paul's agenda that day. He didn't appeal, so maybe there was something to be said for the direct approach.

Jerry did, however, have a marginally better excuse than the lad who was caught grazing on scotch eggs in the warehouse. Another investigation and disciplinary meeting followed. 'Why did you do it?' I asked. 'Dunno!' he replied lethargically. 'I don't even like 'em.' Seriously.

On another occasion, a warehouse operative nicked a whopping big case of shampoo. It was allegedly intercepted on its way to a local car boot sale. John, the warehouse manager, was suitably entertained by this one as the employee in question struggled to justify walking off the site with the box balanced on his head; subtle wasn't this lad's strong point. 'Well, it brings a whole new meaning to 'Wash 'n Go' doesn't it lad?'

It wasn't just the warehouse operatives that were helping themselves to Pricetown's property. As the controller of the canteen's budget (naturally), I had to make sure that we were spending within allocation each month or I'd have to face a painful and profoundly patronising inquisition from Lindsey. Doing anything I could to avoid that, I meticulously went through the spend each month with Doreen, the jovial and always warm canteen manager.

Our outsourced catering company had appointed her. One particular month, we noticed a considerable spike in the cost of replacing cutlery and crockery and a coinciding dip in revenue generated from vending machines. CCTV was put into the kitchen and dining areas. It made interesting viewing, better than an episode of 'Frost'.

Firstly, we discovered that one of the kitchen assistants was partial to wrapping up full sets of cutlery and crockery in one of the crisp, white linen tablecloths that we saved for Christmas and big events. When questioned, she said she'd been looking for an engagement present for her sister and this stuff would do nicely - at our expense. She even went into great detail of how she'd covered her three-piece-suite in the tablecloths, thus transforming her living quarters when she placed a couple of colourful cushions on the chairs. I was pleased for her, on an aesthetic level and intrigued by her openness when questioned, but clearly, she had to go.

Next, we found that people on the night shifts had a penchant for upending the vending machines. The produce would fall out of the bottom; explaining the excessive number of times we had to call engineers out. To add insult to injury, we were also getting accused by the employees that we weren't providing adequate machines. One good shake could feed half a dozen people for the night. The weird thing was they also did this to the hot drinks machine, which contained powdered tea, coffee, soup and juice. It was all subsidised, so the drinks only cost 10p per cup. It turns out that these cups have a good retail value at non-league football grounds and kids' football games on Sunday mornings. Who knew?

As I said, I didn't take any pleasure in people getting caught, or in the subsequent investigations, disciplinary meetings, dismissals and appeals that inevitably followed, running these processes was part of the job but some of the reasons people gave were highly amusing.

Putting aside the fact that no two days are the same in HR, a lot of the days had the same look and feel to them. On a more sombre and sobering note, sometimes something random and unexpected would happen. We just had to hope that initiative, common sense, the odd bit of blind panic and a lot of luck would combine to provide an acceptable outcome.

One such occasion involved Bob, one of our warehouse operators, a driver called Tommy and an admin assistant called June. Bob and June were married and had been for some time. The two of them, along with Tommy's wife Paula were quite close, socialising regularly. Bingo every Friday for the ladies, Crown and Cushion for a few games of pool for the lads. Saturdays might involve a curry, a trip to the local or the occasional big night out in town. They lived opposite each other and their kids went to the same school - that kind of close. For whatever reason, June had taken a shine to Tommy and vice versa. The two had been engaged in an extra-marital affair for months before declaring undying love for each other. Bob found out when Paula caught them making out on her antimacassars when she'd popped out to the greenhouse for some vine tomatoes. This did not go down well, as you might imagine.

From a Harfield perspective, Bob and Tommy mostly worked the early shift together, which started at 6.00 a.m. I'd sometimes get calls from shift managers around this time as they were finishing night shifts or starting day shifts, so I wasn't altogether surprised to see a call from Tom early in the day.

"Morning, Tom," I said chirpily.

"Never mind that. Tommy Doherty's been stabbed at work! Get over here pronto. The place is crawling with coppers."

"Stabbed?" I asked incredulously. Snapping out of it quickly I said, "Yes, of course. Do we know if he's ok?"

"Not sure, he's in the ambulance now. It wasn't pretty and the walls in the main corridor are a nice shade of crimson. Get here as soon as you can. I might need you to do a press release."

I hot-footed it over to the site and was only allowed access by the police when I explained my role and how I could help with next of kin details for the alleged victim and support for any of our employees who had seen it happen. It turned out that, under threat of physical harm from Paula, June had confessed all to Bob at home the previous evening. She told him that she was planning to run into the Mancunian sunset with Tommy. Bob had been shocked and upset at the revelation; he'd had a restless night but had calmly left for work, as usual, the following morning. Only this time, he had furnished himself with a hammer and knife from his toolkit and had snuggly stuffed them into his pockets. Perhaps regrettably, we weren't in the habit of searching employees on their way into the premises, just on the way out. This practice came under review later.

Bob had dutifully arrived at work and had immediately charged over to the transport office clutching his hammer. He was looking for Tommy and looking for trouble. Bob was mad for it. Fortunately for Tommy, he wasn't there. The only manager around was John who had been on a night shift. Upon hearing shouting, he came out from the warehouse to see what was going on. Still wielding his hammer, Bob broke down in tears and explained the situation. John duly took him for a cup of hot sugary tea and tried to calm him down. John listened for a good while whilst Bob poured out his heart and soul regarding recent events. He counselled Bob that whilst it was a shock to find out that your wife was having an affair with one of your closest friends, it was a step too far to charge around work with a hammer in your hand looking for retribution. John did his best to convey that this sort of activity could only lead to disaster and more heartache for all concerned.

Encouragingly, Bob seemed to understand John's point. "I know all that!" he cried, "but I just want to kill him. He's one of my best mates and I'm going to miss him when they go off together."

"What? You'll miss *him* more than your wife?" John asked incredulously.

"Yeah, I reckon so. He's still a twat though and

I'm really mad at him. Well, both of them really, but this will completely knacker our Saturday afternoons at the football and I'm pissed off about that. Also, we're three games off being crowned pool champions in our local league. Dirty bastard."

In a very unfortunately misjudged moment, John thought that Bob was calm enough to go about his business and naively sent him on his way. Bob thanked John for the chat and the much-needed brew and made his way to the locker room to start work.

Only John hadn't joined the dots properly and failed to take the hammer from Bob. Nor did John realise that there might still be a risk of Bob bumping into Tommy whilst on shift that morning. To top it all (and arguably there's no way he could have known this), John did not understand that Bob also had a knife in his pocket as well as the hammer that he'd brought in to work.

Unfortunately, as he made his way towards the locker room, Bob saw Tommy on the stairs ahead of him. He duly whacked him on the side of the head with the hammer and proceeded to shove him down the stairs where he fell on the landing, forming a contorted, almost foetal ball shape. Seizing his chance to do more damage, he started to slash Tommy across his back with the knife, before eventually being pulled away by others who were in the vicinity. In the commotion, Bob took to his heels.

Bob had done a lot of damage in a short space of time. His frenzy meant that Tommy was in a mess, as were the walls, floor and anyone who had helped him or tried to provide first aid before the ambulance arrived. The police made it to the site first and blockaded it, both to stop anyone coming in and also prevent Bob from getting out. The rest of the area was evacuated as the hunt for Bob got underway.

After a short search, he was found hiding in one of the freezers at a cool 24 degrees below. Ironically, he was eating an ice pop at the time of his capture. Bob was promptly charged and escorted off-site. He subsequently pleaded guilty to causing grievous bodily harm after narrowly avoiding a charge of attempted murder on the grounds of diminished responsibility. He was sentenced to twenty-four months in prison but was out for good behaviour after a year. Luckily, Tommy recovered, but it took a while and he had to have a good few weeks off work. We did, of course, offer counselling to all concerned, making sure that everyone was ok after witnessing the incident and the resulting bloodshed.

During our investigation and after the event, Tom tried to understand why John had let Bob go without taking the hammer off him. I know that hindsight is a wonderful thing, but I had to agree with Tom that this should have been at the front of John's mind when he was with Bob. John explained that at the time, he thought that Bob had calmed down sufficiently enough to go and start work. He had the impression that Bob knew that he had done the wrong thing and that he had just had a moment of madness. He was usually a steady away, quiet type. In all honesty, I think that it had slipped John's mind. I guess you don't know how you would react in the same circumstances but, as Tom had articulated, this one should have been fairly obvious.

Tom was persistent in his endeavours to find an explanation and asked a series of quick-fire questions to John along the following lines:

'Did you know that Bob had a hammer about his person?'

'Why didn't you confiscate it?'

'Did you not think to check for other potential weapons?'

'Why the chuff did you not call the police when you had the chance man? All of this might have been prevented if you'd just used your noggin!'

John provided frank answers in a very sheepish manner, clearly understanding that perhaps he should have done things differently. Tom was in an unforgiving mood. He was very lucid in his expectations should an incident of this nature happen in the future.

"Let me be clear, John," he offered in his most military voice (which didn't quite scream 'armed forces' but he was most sincere). "If anything like this happens again, God forbid, you must isolate that employee. Lock them in a bloody office if you must and then call the police. Ring Gemma straight after that."

I must have flashed him a strange look, not realising that I was top of the communication and decision-making tree (as well as media handling) when it came to emergencies and crises on site. Neither did I think my name was on the operating licence for the whole business, but I guess I was being promoted. Seeing my face, Tom quickly added, "Or me, if you must, but Gemma's good at dealing with unforeseen nightmares like this."

A compliment too - the most direct feedback I'd ever received to that point in my career. John solemnly promised to remember this vital process as Tom muttered something about completing the paperwork for the HSE (Health and Safety Executive) and how top brass at Harfield as well as Pricetown were all over the case. Not to mention 'the bloody scavengers from the local rag' for whom I had to prepare a bland and mundane statement, giving nothing away.

Off Tom went. I checked that John was ok. Despite him making a huge faux pas, I knew that he'd be feeling hugely responsible. The scenes he had witnessed had been pretty horrific, from a blood loss point of view. It had been a sizeable clean-up operation, as well as having had a broad impact on the employees, friends and colleagues of Bob and Tommy. I also spoke with Paula and June to advise them what had happened. I was the point of liaison with the police at the scene and with investigations afterwards. I hadn't been there when it had happened and felt that we had a duty of care to John, as well as those who had seen it all as it unfolded and tried to help Tommy in his hour of need.

John puffed out his cheeks, declared that he was fine and that a 'chippy tea' would help him to relax. Excellent, I wouldn't want anything to come between him and his mushy peas.

Fast forward a few weeks. My phone was ringing - at 5.15 in the morning. It's never good news when that happens. It was John. "Hello?" I croaked, trying to sound like I'd been up for hours. "Morning love, It's John. There's been another incident," he said nervously.

"Oh God, what's happened now? Is everyone safe and well? Are you ok?" My heart rate suddenly increased ten-fold.

"Aye love, everything is under control," said John, with a tinge of pride in his voice. "The thing is, I've caught a lad stealing a box of Mr Kipling's country slices on the early shift. I've tied him to a chair, wrapped him in duck-tape from head to foot and locked him in the security hut until the coppers arrive. I've left holes for him to breathe through. I thought you'd want to know straight away. There's no way he'll be doing any more damage today!"

"Amazing!" said I.

Chapter 7

Safety First From Now On - Well, Mostly!

One area where the union was particularly influential was Health and Safety; unless you were Jason in his swivel chair. Most companies I ever worked for had a 'safety first' approach to running the business. In pro-active union environments, the elected safety representatives usually attended the recognised union's health and safety training courses - a good thing, especially when reviewing accidents and looking at disciplinary issues. However, sometimes the reps would use the knowledge they had learned as a stick to beat the business with - especially if they weren't keen on their line manager.

An example of this would be refusing to carry out a procedure on the grounds of health and safety. More often than not, the concerns raised were genuine. Still, suppose a team leader, supervisor or a particular warehouse manager had spoken to someone in the wrong way or union reps wanted to prove a point. In that case, they could cause the operation to stop, at least temporarily. If they reported a health or safety problem, they knew that work would cease in that area to carry out an investigation. Here was another reason why employee relations were so important. Any breach could be used as a tool for unofficial industrial action - just like the previously mentioned barbecue scenario. Furthermore, any employee who expressed an interest in becoming a safety representative would undergo training through the recognised union. They would return from the courses armed with knowledge and would not be afraid to use it!

The Union and Safety representatives quite rightly held the management team accountable for running a safe workplace. As such, we held regular joint Safety Committee Meetings with an 'Action Item Register' with those accountable listed against the agreed actions. We had 'Accident Review Meetings', to see how we could improve safety and, my personal favourite - walking around the site with reps to spot potential risks and conduct safety audits. They enjoyed pointing things out that should have been fixed weeks ago but shied away from answering difficult questions like why there was a pile of empty beer cans in the boiler room.

In general, we had an unspoken understanding that if something happened related to health and safety, then it was dealt with quickly, in the best interests of all concerned. These events sometimes worked in favour of management in disciplinary situations like when Rory O'Malley was caught smoking next to the fuel pumps. Rory wasn't the sharpest tool in the box. He'd dabbled at being an employee rep at various stages, which can be a challenging role at times, but even his membership thought he was 'too thick' for re-election. Their words, not mine. Harsh.

We'd known for a while that someone (or perhaps several people, given the mountains of Lambert & Butler tabs found in the area) was taking the opportunity to maximise their smoking breaks on the night shift. It was easier to get away with more on 'nights' and everyone knew it. Most of this had been relatively innocuous, like having slightly longer breaks than they should, ordering a curry to work and the occasional stripper for birthdays; these were occasions where we could turn a blind eye. However, smoking next to tanks of fuel was not one of those occasions.

At the time, it was still socially acceptable to smoke in pubs and specified areas at work; it would be a good few years before the ban on smoking in the workplace came into effect. After some discussion, Paul and I decided to gather people together in groups on the shop floor to explain the hazards of smoking in non-designated areas, which perhaps should have been obvious. Rory looked after the place where the fuel was stored, but it didn't necessarily follow that a driver was our culprit. The CCTV didn't stretch to the area in question and Tom was reluctant to ask Pricetown for money for this as it would highlight that we had a problem with smoking on site.

So, having briefed Paul on the reasons we were doing this, we got all those concerned together and I kicked off proceedings. I started by explaining that we accepted that people wanted to smoke but that we had provided specific areas for this in the interest of health and safety. The people doing this were putting themselves and their colleagues at risk, so we needed to follow the rules before anyone was seriously hurt, or worse. The majority of people got the message but, for the avoidance of doubt, Paul added his brand of motivation for the troops, Wigan accent in full flow.

'What Gemma is saying is that some dickhead round here is smoking next to the fuel pumps and tankers. Smoking here is a foolish thing to do unless you want to end up looking like a melted fucking welly. Whoever it is, needs to stop, pronto. When I catch them, they will get such a large fucking rocket up their shitty arsehole that it will make Apollo 13 look like a crap firework. Is that crystal fucking clear? Seriously, it needs to stop. Don't be a dickhead. Just be normal.'

I couldn't envisage Paul fronting a government campaign anytime soon, but I think most people got the message. Alex and Jason came up to me at the end of the briefing and told me they'd keep an ear out. I knew they'd never 'grass', but as long as it stopped, I didn't mind too much.

So, after a few more weeks of investigation, we concluded that cigarette butts were only ever found when Rory was seen approaching the fire door that led to the area on the internal CCTV. I called Jason and John in to say that we needed to show him the evidence and speak with him. The plan was to ask him directly as he came onto shift that evening. We would show him the footage and ask to look in his locker for cigarettes that matched those found. I asked Paul to wait with me in my office as Jason said he would bring Rory up for the investigation meeting to commence.

They took a while to arrive, but when they did, I was surprised to see a vitriolic John and a sopping wet Rory, covered in foam. He asked for the eyewash from the first aid kit. We cleaned him up and asked them what had happened.

"We caught him in the act," said John. "Just as he was flicking a red-hot fag end towards the tanker truck. So, I decided to extinguish it and him along with it." He was nothing if not enthusiastic these days.

"Right, well let's get you cleaned up and dried off and then we'll get into the details. I'll grab you a clean uniform and you can get showered." Rory looked fleetingly grateful in his state of shock.

"I've got a spare ball and chain in my locker," piped up Jason, licking his lips slightly. "Single cuff. Shall I go and grab it, to make sure he doesn't try and escape the penance coming his way?"

"Erm, no, I don't think that will be necessary." I replied, making a mental note to ask him 'why' next time I spoke with him.

So, Rory cleaned himself up and we cleaned out his eye. He knew that what he was doing was wrong. He just couldn't be bothered walking to the smoking shelters or designated Portacabins as they were a good couple of minutes away from his workstation. He said he knew it was dangerous, but he hadn't had any accidents to date, so maybe it was ok to carry on. It was a no brainer and we came to a mutual agreement that he would resign as opposed to going through a gross misconduct disciplinary process. It seemed crackers to me that someone would lose their job for the sake of walking a few feet, but there was no option about the outcome owing to the dangerous nature of his lethargy. Rory had to go.

John had to source a new fire extinguisher for the area in question and answer to his new nickname of 'Fireman Sam' for the foreseeable future. Jason had to have a word with himself about bringing medieval weaponry to work. Paul was convinced that he always knew 'we'd catch the bastard sooner or later'. Life went on.

The aforementioned walk-around audits were very effective. They relied on people reporting things correctly, conducting the audits with regular cadence and any issues being dealt with swiftly. I also liked them because they provided a good reason to walk around the shop floor, check-in with people and see what life was like at the coal face. I didn't mind getting togged up in safety boots, PPE and hi-vis vests to conduct those audits, but not all of my colleagues felt the same way.

Take Lindsey in Accounts, for example. No, please take her! One day, much to her dismay she was up against it in terms of workload - it always seemed to be either month-end, period end, quarter-end, year-end or indeed 'bell end', as Paul Tetley would have it. It appeared to be every other day in Accounts. Despite her having a 'much more significant and more pressurised workload' than anyone else, Lindsey reluctantly undertook her safety audit of the main assembly lines with Jason and another safety rep in tow. What Lindsey didn't know is that a couple of the warehouse lads, let's call them Dick and Harry, had an ongoing mission to 'out-prank' each other with various innocuous tricks and acts of horseplay. For weeks they'd been hiding each other's lunches, putting salt in each other's brews and leaving 'gifts' in each other's lockers (you can imagine the guise that these gifts took). Just as poor Lindsey approached the last of the aisles, Dick jumped out of a four-foot mailbag screaming 'Gertcha' at, who he thought was, Harry, passing by. Lindsey's clipboard jumped out of her hands, flying into the air at lightning speed. She also, simultaneously let out a very audible fart and a loud scream. Rumour had it that she expended a little wee, as she hurried away in horror.

A detailed investigation had to be undertaken. I had to keep a straight face and interview all parties. The first I heard about it was when Paul popped his head through my office door and announced that 'Chanel Knickers has pissed herself in the warehouse and not in a good way. No kinky shit, just pure pissed herself'. I didn't stop to ask if there was ever a right way to piss yourself at work or what 'kinky shit' could possibly relate to (each to their own after all). We simply shared a wry smile. I put my best-concerned face on and went to find Lindsey so that both the investigation and healing processes could begin in tandem.

Other items that we might look at together from a Management / Union / Safety perspective included the phantom turd leaver. Not really an HR issue, strictly speaking, but Tom tasked me with 'getting to the bottom of this shite' (apt choice of words) and find out who exactly was leaving the gift of a floating turd in trap one of the men's toilets every Monday morning, without fail. As far as Tom was concerned, this was becoming a distraction, with employees and supervisors alike focusing more and more on the floater than on the Monday morning production meeting; it had to stop. Everything came to a head one Monday morning when Tom caught Liz and Paul outside the men's toilet with a flag in their hands.

"What are you doing?" asked Tom, knowing that something was amiss.

"Nothing, nothing at all," replied Paul and Liz in suspicious unison.

"So why is Liz hanging out around the men's loos and why are you carrying a flag?" questioned

Tom.

"Well… erm given that we're struggling to find the owner of the recurring turd," began Paul.

"We thought we'd pay our respects instead and stick a flag in it," said Liz.

"Woah, woah, woah, sweet baby Jesus and the orphans!" exclaimed a horrified Tom. "What if someone sees you two hanging around a toilet together? Folk have been arrested for less. Get back to work right now and forget all this nonsense. We need to sort 'Turdgate' once and for all. I'm going to give this to Gemma as a mini-project," he blustered.

I was next on Tom's walk around. I persuaded him that putting out a communication on the tannoy or issuing a notice instructing people to 'Fucking Flush' might not be the most subtle way to address it. We compromised on 'Polite Notices' on the back of each toilet door asking people to flush away their offerings, leave the toilet in a condition that they would like to find it and wash their hands.

Tom still wanted to find the person so that he could ask them 'Why in God's name would you do such a thing?' Needless to say, our investigations did not prove fruitful. I have to say, that on a medical, or even human level, the size of these offerings led me to conclude that we either had a well-disguised woolly mammoth working in the building or someone was giving birth to medium-sized lizard-like reptiles at work. Some of them had the look and hue of a very poorly iguana and if we ever did track down the former owner, my first thought would have been to refer them for medical attention.

Elsewhere, we introduced ergonomic assessments, which included manual handling training on the shop floor to make lifting, moving, bending and carrying more manageable and safer. We engaged the services of an independent company, HSE Solutions, to help us with this. In the offices, it included a desk, chair, monitor and posture checks to make sure that employees didn't unnecessarily sustain repetitive strain injuries or back and neck problems. Alongside this came company-funded eye tests for anyone using a VDU (Visual Display Unit) and more funding for occupational health services on site.

All in all, managers and employees saw this as a good thing and supported the various initiatives taking place. Liz, however, was a bit put out when Mike from HSE Solutions had the audacity to suggest she was sitting too close to her screen and that her elbows weren't at the right height. He declared that with an adjustment to her chair; tilting the angle of her monitor and the placing of a footstool would improve things. His mistake was in warning Liz against the perils of doing nothing, which could impact her movement and flexibility in the long term.

"Flexibility?" scoffed Liz as she rounded on poor Mike. "I'll have you know that I do yoga, pilates and pole dancing classes three times a week." With this, she stood up from her chair, jumped over her desk and strutted towards Mike. By this stage, he was walking backwards, nervously towards Liz's office door. She continued, "Other things you should know, before you start making assumptions and pissing on my very agile parade, include the fact that I have a core of steel. I can get my legs in places usually only accessible to octopuses and other similar invertebrates!"

With arguably predatory connotations, she pinned poor Mike up against the wall, placing one foot on his shoulder. With that, she made a 'grrrrrrrr' sound and invited him to skedaddle out of her office. He duly did so, at much speed. The poor man was terrified. We all thought it was hilarious when Liz re-enacted the event in a management meeting, an over-excited Tony Slater playing the role of Mike. For the record, Tony's hair colour was a warm amber with hints of autumn and he relished every moment of his role.

There were times when we had to investigate accidents in the workplace, some occasions more straightforward than others. We trained supervisors and team leaders to complete accident forms and conduct necessary investigations. The management team would only need to get involved in reviewing the findings or when things progressed to a disciplinary matter and someone was at fault.

We had occasions where someone suffered severe trauma, such as 'de-gloving' of a finger (where extensive sections of skin are torn away from the underlying tissue) because they hadn't followed the correct LOTO (lockout, tag out) procedures on specific machinery. We had occasions where people slipped on the floor, injuring their backs. Technically it was the fault of the company for not making sure that areas were clean, tidy or hazard-free. We needed to own up to when we'd been at fault and make things safer for everyone.

Perhaps the most intriguing accidents of all were the ones that happened with no rhyme or reason and where no one was seriously hurt. There were ones that left you completely dumbfounded, like how the fork-lift truck driver could drive head-first into a luminous pink pillar that had been recently painted to help people avoid it. Or how someone could trip over a pallet that they had placed on the floor themselves, resulting in a week off work with a bruised knee and subsequent personal injury claim form. And for the record, no, we didn't keep documents in HR that people could use to help them sue the company. It seemed pretty straightforward to me, but it didn't stop them asking!

One of the most bizarre 'alleged' accidents happened under the ever-watchful eye of warehouse manager John. It wasn't an accident at all but had to be investigated and reported as such. Following budgetary and operational approval, John asked one of the maintenance technicians, Dave Sparky, to increase the width and height of the loading bay archways for ease of access to the 'goods in' and 'goods out' areas. Unbeknown to John, Dave was having some mental health issues of his own, having gambled away his life savings on reverse forecast doubles at Belle Vue. John went through the plans for the work with Dave, then dutifully cordoned off the area so that Dave and his maintenance colleagues could begin the challenging structural dismantling.

Despite being armed with all the right tools to commence work, Dave thought it would be more efficient to climb his stepladder and give the roof of the first loading bay a bash with his lump hammer. Once the first joists and brickwork came loose, he aimed to head-butt his way around the rest of the construction. A gathering of his colleagues started to form as he 'nutted' his way around the structure with his seemingly well-hard forehead. People, including Alex and safety reps that were in the area, urged him to stop. They were being covered in debris and, eventually, blood from Dave's extremely furrowed brow.

Ultimately, I received a phone call from John, who explained that Dave was 'hitting his head against a brick wall'. I thought it was a euphemism at first, so I implored John to give him some words of encouragement and alternative suggestions that might help him complete the task in hand. It was only when he said, "No love, you don't understand. He is literally twatting his head against the brickwork and he won't stop. He'll be unconscious soon."

I hastily donned my hi-vis vest and PPE, hot-footed it to the area, pushed my way to the front of the watching crowd and implored him to stop. It was only when I said, "Whatever the problem is, whatever the issue, we will help you - you're not on your own at all," that he paused for breath and calmed a little. I softly encouraged him to come down and get cleaned up, promised him some privacy and a cuppa away from the madness and a listening ear. He subsequently opened up about how much debt he was in, how, as a result, he was in danger of losing his car, his house and his marriage. We put him in touch with the right agencies so that he could get help with his gambling addiction and debt management. I managed to persuade Tom that the right thing to do in this one-off case would be to give him an emergency loan to pay off some initial and immediate debts. He paid this back to the business weekly, without interest. It was at this point that I started to think that we needed a more robust process and framework to assist employees who were carrying heavy burdens. It didn't matter whether they were work-related or not - I felt that we owed it to people to help where we could, but more on that later.

Whilst it was enshrined in law that we had a duty of care to everyone on-site, we couldn't always account for the inadequacies of contractors or visitors to the distribution centre. When two of our esteemed suppliers came to site one day, it transpired that they had met before and found themselves unable to keep their hands off each other in the elevator when suddenly the lift broke down. It was apparent that they had engaged in some rather rambunctious rumpy-pumpy whilst trapped inside. They'd had time to compose themselves and arrange their attire by the time the engineers rescued them but failed to hide the condom we later found in the corner of the lift. Gross, I thought as it landed on my desk in a clear plastic bag (I was grateful for the bag!) from a traumatised maintenance employee, but at least they'd practised safe sex, I guess. The impact of their passionate exchange rendered the lift 'out of action'. A contractor came one fateful weekend to fix the damage.

The lift doors were stuck open on one of the floors and access to the shaft was visible. The scene was cordoned off with some red and white 'crime scene' tape. Arguably, it was enough for sensible folk to realise something wasn't right and steer clear, but it was inadequate for the more curious, or those people who were maybe not blessed with an abundance of grey matter.

One such person was Jason, union rep extraordinaire. Ignoring the haphazardly placed tape, he was poking around the lift shaft with some sort of implement on the Sunday night shift; well after the contractors had gone home. Lord only knows which instrument of torture he had used to try and satisfy his curiosities, but he managed to dislodge something which sent the main lift compartment crashing straight to the bottom of the lift shaft. Fortunately, it crashed with a thunderous bang, prompting John, who was on shift that night, to leave his cup of tea to go cold in the canteen and investigate. He duly found Jason clinging to the edge of the elevator shaft, perilously close to dropping to the floor himself.

"What are you doing man?" exclaimed John as he dragged Jason to safety.

"Well, I just fell into this position whilst conducting my investigations," said Jason.

"I think you might just have over-stepped your remit again sunshine, as well as the red tape around the place. What were you thinking?"

Cue a phone call to me. I was engaged in a game of pool on Quiz Night with Matt and some friends; a wild ritual that we had back then on a Sunday evening. I contacted the Maintenance Manager, who was on call for such events and between him and John, they made sure that the area was safe. I asked John to take a statement from Jason and made sure that he requested Jason's presence at a meeting the following evening to explain what had happened. Jason wasn't happy, blaming the contractor for not having adequate barriers to the danger zone.

"Whoever that contractor is he ought to suffer the 'Pear of Anguish' for this and then the 'Iron Maiden'!" Jason exclaimed. In the subsequent meeting, he protested his innocent involvement in a significant health and safety incident. Neither I, John or Bobby Buck had any idea what he was talking about. I later wished I hadn't found out what the 'Pear of Anguish' was, as will you if you choose to google it. As for the 'Iron Maiden', I wholeheartedly wanted to run to the hills after discovering what that was used for.

Meanwhile, the contracting company were informed, but they couldn't have cared less. In their view, red tape was adequate and Jason was an idiot for disregarding it. They had a valid point, but they could have secured the area better by creating a more robust cordon so that this could have been avoided. Suffice to say, we didn't use their services again.

As for the two suitors who had caused this in their moment of passion, they ended up married, had twins and were divorced within the space of twelve months. Fast work seemed to be their thing.

Overall, in the UK, we were experiencing a new phase of tighter regulations, coupled with a raised awareness of health, safety and well-being at work, albeit at the early stage of its evolution. Legislation in the UK was becoming tighter concerning personal injury claims, making it much easier for employees to sue employers for work-related accidents and rightly so. We did a lot of work to create a 'Safety First' culture at Harfield Distribution. In all honesty, we were better than most when it came to honouring our duty of care to employees, providing safe systems of work, PPE and training. We tried to encourage employees to report 'near misses' as well as actual accidents so that the right procedures could be changed or put in place before a serious accident happened. The mantra was that no one ever got in trouble for reporting a near-miss, they were often congratulated for doing so as it could have prevented something serious from happening. On the other hand, you might well be in bother if it came to light that you knew about something precarious and carried on working regardless or failed to report it. This approach seemed fair as it was in everyone's best interest to raise concerns and clearly, reporting actual accidents was a must.

Be that as it may, did I report the accident - or not so near miss - when I slipped on the back staircase, snapping the heel of my precious new court shoe, then skidded on my arse straight into the men's toilets at the bottom of the said flight of steps? Never in a month of Sundays! I cautiously stood up, checked no one had seen, dusted off my power suit, vigorously rubbed my bruised, but pert, twenty-something derriere, cursed my wretched, broken court shoe and tottered off for lunch. Enough said.

Chapter 8

THE ROLLERCOASTER OF LIFE

Life throws all sorts at you - as you know.

On the personal front, I was riding high. Matt and I were getting on well; I loved Matt's family and my own family took him to their hearts like another son or brother. We had loads of fun together. He made me laugh, he was a showman and if ever I was under the weather with a cold or the like, he'd think nothing of driving sixty miles over the Pennines on a freezing, wet Tuesday evening to bring me some 'Lemsips'. Then he'd spend the night with me and then drive back at 5.00 a.m. the following morning for work. I knew he was a keeper.

We'd been together for about a year when, one fine day, he proposed. We'd taken a break from the usual routine and had gone to Liverpool. Whilst we were technically in Liverpool, Matt's romantic proposal was made with one leg hanging off the Isle of Wight whilst clinging desperately onto Portsmouth!

Let me explain. Some of you may recall the wobbly floating wonder, namely 'Fred's Weather Map' at Albert Dock in Liverpool. It was used every day on the TV programme 'This Morning' for weather updates and it featured on 'Granada Reports' (ITV's regional news) for many years in the North West. Weather presenter, Fred Talbot, would skip and jump across a large-scale map of the UK that was tethered to the bed of the Irish Sea, just off the edge of the dock. It was a well-known feature on British television at the time, as was Fred Talbot. This was years before he faced criminal charges for two counts of indecent sexual assault and was sentenced to five years in prison. He didn't feature on daytime TV after that and his map was confined to the TV archive.

Back to more innocent days... as students, Matt and I would watch Fred, glued to 'This Morning' during the day and at night we watched him while eating our supper. Fred enthusiastically hopped all over the British Isles predicting the weather for the viewers at home. I think he had a captive audience. We were all waiting with bated breath to see if he would fall into the sea whilst jumping from Scotland to Northern Ireland and back again via the Isle of Man.

Ignoring the feeble-looking chain designed to stop visitors and tourists jumping onto the map (Fred must have had a plank or something to help him board and alight), Matt tried to jump onto the south coast of England. He was successful with his upper body and arms, but sadly one leg landed on the Isle of Wight whilst the other one missed and went into the water. His arms clung on to Pompey for dear life as he managed to bark a hurried, 'Will you marry me?' Security arrived and we were escorted from the premises. We would eventually look back and laugh, once we'd completed a statement, had mugshots taken, been asked never to return and shopped for new, dry, clean clothes before arriving at the pub for pie 'n' mash. Naturally, I said yes.

Life's rich tapestry also stretched to the world of HR. One minute you can be offering someone a job and the next investigating why a guy would want to wee up an outside wall when the toilets were just inside. Most situations are pretty straightforward when you break them down; they become routine or part of the job. Once in a while, though, something or someone will come along and you know that you'll remember them forever. They will etch an indelible emotional impression upon you that will change the way you look at things forever. Even just thinking of the name Paul Garvey does this for me.

I had come to think of Harfield as one big family. Ok, a pretty dysfunctional family, but one with a strong sense of loyalty and love at the heart of it. On the outer ring roads of major northern cities, with redundant industrial mills as a backdrop, it was commonplace for generation after generation of the same family to work at companies like Harfield. Social problems, crime and broken families were prevalent, yet somehow coming to work provided a grounding framework. It didn't take me long to realise that if Mick slandered Gary in the warehouse in 'Goods-In', there would suddenly appear at least two of Gary's half-brothers, one of Gary's second cousins, half removed and Gary's formidable great aunt Sheila. They'd offer the slanderer a sharp, swift slap for berating 'our Gary', thus sending a powerful message that they were not to be messed with.

This sense of family brings me to brothers Paul and Keith, two of Harfield's best warehouse workers. They were grafters who consistently worked hard to earn an honest crust. Keith was the older of the two and was fiercely protective of Paul, who was stone deaf. However, Paul could lip-read with no problems. This skill was used to great effect when Paul saw people saying things they shouldn't, thinking he couldn't hear them.

'That Tony Slater is a right wanker!' people would often say in what they thought were hushed tones.

'He is, isn't he?' Paul would reply, much to their amazement.

Paul was popular because he was one of the lads. He got on with his work and never made a big deal out of being deaf. If it were up to him, he wouldn't mention it at all. Paul had a great sense of family, wanting to work hard for his wife, Amy and their two young children. His deafness had become progressively worse over time owing to an aneurysm near his brain; I was no medic, but my understanding was that this was a bulge in a blood vessel caused by a weakness in its wall. In terms of workplace safety, we needed to be aware of this so that we could provide a safe environment in which to work. This meant regular meetings and check-ins with HR and Occupational Health.

Paul, in his stoic manner, repeatedly told me that most aneurysms don't even show symptoms and are not dangerous. However, given that his was growing slowly and steadily, Paul was keen to have an operation that would tackle it. Another plus side to this was that it could potentially solve the 'bloody nuisance' (Paul's words) of his hearing loss.

It doesn't take a rocket scientist to imagine why working in a warehouse environment when you are deaf is a pretty significant hazard. We had occupational health in early to assess Paul's needs and provide a support programme. Little changes were introduced, which could become big things in a given situation, such as assigned fire marshals to locate Paul in the event of a fire. He had multiple contacts in HR, Occupational Health and among his shift managers, to whom he could speak at any point. He was given lots of smaller, more regular or 'split' work to do, as opposed to bulk orders, so that the supervisors and team leaders could check in on him more regularly than others for safety reasons. He worked with a good crew and was generally very happy with his lot.

In addition to my regular, more formal check-ins with Paul, sometimes I'd just grab him for a coffee and we'd have a chat on the bench outside. He was an easy-going character and nothing bothered him too much; he had a wife, a son and daughter and just wanted to take care of them financially and emotionally. He would share his worries with me about not being able to continue working one day. But he was determined to work for as long as he could. The thing he wanted most of all was an operation to 'clip' his aneurysm whilst undergoing an open craniotomy – a procedure not without risk. Eventually, after much consultation and many months of waiting, Paul's operation date came through.

I was rooting for Paul in a way I can't put into words. I'd got to know him and his family well. His resilience in the face of the lot that he'd been dealt was second to none. Every operation can, of course, have its complications, but Paul checked in with me every day in the weeks building up to it and he just couldn't wait to get it done. I was fully up to speed on his pre-op appointments and he brought me letters from the hospital and his consultants to keep us updated. I knew from this information that Paul's enlarged artery was considered to be a 'giant aneurysm' and hence it affected his hearing. He told me that because of its size and where it was, there was a greater chance of it rupturing, which would have potentially fatal consequences. For Paul, the obvious (and only) choice was surgery. He calmly shared statistics such as there being a 60% survival rate and that out of the successful operations, 66% of survivors had some form of defect or neurological impact. These statistics were worrying to me, but this was all about Paul and his choices. His calm pragmatism was infectious. He was convinced that it would go smoothly; the only time he welled up was when he spoke of his wife Amy and her desperation for a time without worry. As a full-time mum, her world centred on Paul and the kids. She'd confided in me that she'd feel 'so free' knowing that he'd be able to hear his kids' voices again. Paul was slightly more direct, saying it would open up changes to family life that were 'fucking awesome Gem!'

I wasn't sure if it was because I was young and new to the grown-up world, but I was wholly invested in Paul, his family, his operation, his recovery and his chances of living a normal life when it was all over. Not only did I spend extra time with him at work leading up to the surgery, mostly drinking coffee and chatting about his plans for after the surgery, but Liz and I went to visit his family. Liz had known the children when they were growing up, so various baby stories flew between them and our connection with this family grew and grew. We made sure that Keith knew that we were there for him at work as well.

There were some difficult conversations to be had with Paul and Amy but nobody feared the worst. Still, Paul had wanted to know that his family would be financially secure should the operation not go according to plan. I had to pull together and share information about the death in service payments, life assurance and dismissals relating to incapacity, with an employee who was still very much alive. I found it most comfortable to discuss this kind of information by going into a factual, pragmatic, accurate mode. Emotions had their place, but giving a man the required details on what his family would be entitled to in the event of his death was not one of them. We were, of course, preparing for every possible eventuality, every possible outcome, but never did the younger version of me ever doubt that he would make it; we were just practical, covering all bases.

The day of the operation came. I made sure that Keith had the day off work with full pay to be at the hospital with Amy. In many other ways, it was work as usual. Paul's operation was on my mind all day, but the world of work keeps moving and soon the time came when I knew that Paul would be in recovery. I'd just finished a meeting with Liz at around 4.00 p.m. and was in her office. She was as keen as I was to hear how the surgery had gone and to know that Paul was ok; I thought nothing of using her phone to ring Amy, safe in the knowledge that it would be a quick, simple update of information.

Only it wasn't. Paul had not made it.

Even though we had, in theory, prepared for this, I don't think I have ever been floored by something as much.

Liz said she knew straight away that something wasn't right. I listened to Amy's sobs in total silence, before finding the words, any words. The fact that I'd turned utterly white gave it all away. I have goosebumps recalling that moment even now.

I spent the next few days with Amy as this had affected a lot of people at Harfield. I was the assigned person to liaise with the family, sort out the financials and plan for the funeral (with departmental managers, as so many of our employees would want to go). Until this point, I'd always been pretty good at keeping work-related situations in a 'work compartment' inside my head, but this felt personal. Maybe I'd allowed myself to become too involved, too invested. I think it was the combination of it being the first time I'd faced anything like this and getting to know Paul and his family so well. It felt rubbish and unfair and it took me some time to even process it.

There was a massive turnout for his big send-off, as anticipated. Afterwards, I had 'Going Underground' by 'The Jam' whirling around my head for days. It turned out that he had planned all the finer details of his funeral before the operation. Despite his fearless optimism, he remained a pragmatist until the end. He even managed to stick two fingers up to death by announcing his arrival, mod punk rock style.

Paul's story hit our workplace hard.

The way everyone came together when the chips were down made me realise the true worth of my dysfunctional family. Workers from all departments, led by the warehouse crew, had rallied around Paul's family and his brother Keith. Soon, a decision was made to raise as much money as possible for Paul's wife and their two young children. An evening of fundraising in memory of Paul was organised, for which we secured the clubhouse at Oldham Athletic football club, as he had been a lifelong supporter. Pricetown kindly donated all manner of cracking prizes; it would have put the Generation Game conveyor belt to shame. Sixty-five-year-old former nun Maureen from admin was over the moon among the TVs, stereo equipment, canteens of cutlery and vouchers. She won a tattoo consultation with David Beckham's very own artist who was based within striking distance of the depot! I'm still not sure how a packet of organic dog biscuits made it to the grand prize table, but Gary from Transport was made up with his prize. He didn't even have a dog!

Paul's colleagues raised a whopping, amazing, generous and brilliant total of £8,000 on that night. We made sure that every single penny went to the family. Furthermore, I managed to persuade Tom that we didn't need the money in the HR budget to refurbish the security hut and add more toilets. Catching him at a moment of weakness at the end of the night, Tom agreed that we could match the money raised, giving Amy £16,000 in total.

Times like these restore your faith in humanity. You can't put a price on how bloody brilliant people can be. I know that the money raised went a long way to easing Amy's immediate financial worries;

she was able to take the kids on a much-needed holiday, giving them time to begin figuring out their life as a family of three. People do care and they show it most when things get tough. The evening in question was a huge tribute to Paul and how well thought of he was, but it was also a great testament to his colleagues. Most of them didn't have much in the way of disposable income, but boy did they pull it out of the bag when it mattered.

Paul's untimely and tragic death made us in HR take stock of how we could further support employees with difficult personal issues. It led to the creation of our 'Employee Assistance Program', something which I remain proud of to this very day. Jan's experience meant that I learned her skill in arguing for items not previously agreed in the department's budget. I'm pretty sure she ganged up on Tom and Lindsey in the end but, whatever, it worked! Very soon, an employee in need would have access to a twenty-four-hour telephone counselling service. This got the workforce talking productively with skilled professionals. The helpline didn't just cover bereavement, but issues such as debt management, relationship difficulties, separation and financial mediation. In short, we were raising the profile of mental health and well-being long before it became the norm.

Of course, first of all, we had to decide which counselling provider to use for the outsourced service. Whilst this was a very serious matter, we had fun finding an appropriate partner. There were quite a few independent counsellors out there claiming to be all things to all people and I soon found out that some of them would have found it difficult to counsel their way out of a Valium factory.

And here is where we met 'Rollercoaster Counsellors - *life is a rollercoaster, learn to ride it with us!*' – our first potential provider. I was the guinea pig as part of the interview process. As an imagined employee, I was to present a fictional issue and David from 'Rollercoaster Counsellors' would respond as he saw fit. Jan would observe, taking notes throughout and was to ask several questions at the end of the mock session, to decide whether or not 'Rollercoaster Counsellors' was right for us.

I had hoped that David would take me on a mild but cathartic 'rollercoaster' ride where we would begin to reflect upon and process some of my imagined 'marital issues'. It turned out that David was on a far more turbulent rollercoaster ride of his own where his marriage was concerned. After only a few sentences, in which I lamented how my husband and I no longer seemed to understand each other, he shifted the attention firmly back onto himself, as, in true professional counsellor style, he disclosed everything to me. Absolutely everything.

Within moments, I knew how often David and his wife had sex; when they first met; their favourite positions and how, whilst he loved his children, he couldn't help resenting their arrival due to a reduction in fellatio at home. I exchanged looks of 'help me!' with Jan, who was sitting behind David. She emitted a barely discernible chortle and then managed to paint her poker face back on. David explained that the disconnect between him and his wife was final when he found it impossible to bring her to climax.

I felt like I was at the very top of 'The Big One' at Blackpool and about to sink into the abyss beneath. As I was pondering this over-share of information, he released a hefty sigh, reached over to the plate of pastries beside us and promptly began to 'comfort-eat' his way through two apple turnovers.

It was safe to say that David from 'Rollercoaster Counsellors' was not a good fit with Harfield's requirements. But at least we were able to give him the contact details of another prospective associate company so that he could seek some professional relationship advice for himself.

Luckily, Kate, from 'Clarity' then graced our doors. Clarity was a larger business with several counsellors employed to offer a corporate service to clients. A consummate professional, Kate was warm and attentive, but never stepped over the line professionally. She always showed a genuine interest in the business and, most importantly, the people she was seeing. Whereas David had launched himself over the line at a fantastic pace, Kate was measured, warm and attentive. In my second experience as an imaginary Harfield

HAVE YOU GOT A MINUTE?

employee, this time as a high-functioning alcoholic (BAFTA would've been calling if I hadn't reined it in), I knew that Kate ('my counsellor') would be a great fit. It felt right that we were going to be able to offer this invaluable service and support to our employees and their dependents, 24/7 – a landmark moment.

Employees like Keith would now be able to access bereavement counselling, something that would have been impossible for him to afford independently. Other employees used the service for all sorts of reasons. Gambling and other addictions were prevalent in the local community. Whether the impact was on our people or their dependants, it was great to know that they had access to professional help.

Legally, it acted as a kind of insurance policy for the business as well, which made Tom sleep easier. We put effort into training managers to watch out for pressure points, warning signs and, if appropriate, helping employees to make that first phone call. Most thought it was great and loved the idea of helping their colleagues. Others were less empathetic.

"What do you mean you're feeling 'stressed'? We're not at war. We're not saving lives. I'm just asking you to shift some boxes from A to B. So, whatever it is, park it for now. When you're at home and in your own time, you can ring the number we've given you and shriek like a stuck pig if you

131

want. Right now, I need that cage of tinned beans with sausage to arrive in Cleckheaton by noon, so crack on lad!"

No prizes for guessing the purveyor of such sage words!

Unfortunately, death has been a recurring theme in the course of my career. Whilst I've never been quite as emotionally steeped in a case as much as I was with Paul, various instances have been tough to process at times. Employee suicides are always incredibly sad and hard to handle. The ramifications across the whole workforce are huge and long-lasting. Desperate feelings of helplessness abound; line managers and colleagues questioning their consciences for months, wondering why they didn't pick up on the signs. In HR, I always felt there was more we could or should have done, but I think the simple fact is that you don't always know what's going on in people's heads or lives. Tragically, for anyone who chooses to end their own life, death seems like the most palatable escape.

In my time, I've had to talk to employees with terminal cancer. I have explained that their loved ones would be better off if they died in service rather than being paid a less valuable redundancy payment whilst still alive. It's a tough conversation to have, but important to ensure that all paperwork is up to date and unnecessary worries allayed. You hold on to the fact that this is what's best for their families; a frank exchange of information is crucial.

As well as being the HR contact for the families concerned, I was the 'Trustee Director' of various pension schemes. I've had to inform a family that a deceased employee had left 50% of their life assurance to a third party, with whom they've fathered a second (and secret) family. On a personal level, watching someone going through the pain of processing grief whilst simultaneously being hit with news like that was not pleasant. Nor was it uncommon. Sometimes people cut their children out of their wills and changed their 'expression of wish' forms at work; leaving everything - including their pension and life assurance - to a new spouse. More often than not, you could see how a new spouse might have manipulated this, following minor disagreements between parent and child, but it certainly wasn't my place to comment.

One time etched on my memory was when I had to personally deliver some tragic news to an employee, rather than the information coming from a police officer. His teenage son had been found dead from a drug overdose in his flat. Geographically, the flat was in a different jurisdiction and therefore not covered by the local police force. Because there weren't enough police officers to travel across county lines to come to site, the earliest they could get to the employee was eight hours later - meeting him at home after work. I didn't think it was right for him to have to continue working for that length of time, not knowing what had happened to his son. It felt wrong that I had this information and he didn't. I'm not sure if the various police forces would even allow this now, let alone ask someone like me to break the news, but, having chatted it through with Jan and Tom, we decided that I should do it; it was a conversation that I would never forget. The employee was utterly grief stricken and his gut-wrenching sobs filled the room until I could make arrangements for him to be escorted home.

I've also learned harsh life lessons when employees have been absent without leave. In the past, we had collectively made several phone calls and sent standard template snotty letters telling them to get in touch or face the consequences. Tragically, it turned out that they had been dead for days; home alone, with no family or friends to notice their absence. These days I allow two hours after the start of someone's working day and then call 111 to make checks. When people accuse me of overreacting, I am unapologetic. I've learned the hard way that all is not always what it seems when dealing with 'fluffy HR shite' such as death.

Going back to the time of Paul's death, I felt proud that we had set up a service that could provide support to our Harfield family. As far as I was concerned, the service was a nod to Paul; his terrible situation had prompted us to explore the different support packages available. It's due to Paul's case and subsequent others, that I remain passionate about providing help and support for people who often spend more time working for Corporate Inc than they do with their own families. It's part of our duty of care as responsible employers; it can help people in dire situations. On a human level, this has to be more important than anything work-related.

Chapter 9

ABSENCE MAKES THE HEART...
TURN TO STONE

Wherever people are employed, there will be absences from work; it is a truth universally acknowledged. In short and from an operational perspective, sickness costs. Statutory sick pay and anything above that, has to be funded by the company. Not only that, cover is needed for the employee who is off ill; a costly set of extra cogs in the absence wheel.

Tom announced that the mammoth £800,000 per year absence bill had come to Pricetown's attention. According to him, 'My cock is firmly on the block and we need to do something about this, pronto'. We embarked on a drive to reduce the cost of absences. Every manager had to be involved and no stone was to be left unturned.

We introduced robust systems for communicating absence and made sure employees were briefed on the requirement to phone their line manager directly. Time was of the essence and had to happen at least one hour before shift start time so that we could plan cover more effectively. That's what the new policy said.

In practice, Paul Tetley's words were, "It is no longer acceptable for your next-door neighbour's cousin's dog to inform me by text that you're not fuckin' coming in. You must phone me yourselves, directly, unless your voice box has fallen out of your arse for some reason. If you do not do this, then you won't be fuckin' paid."

We also explained the importance of keeping in regular touch whilst absent so that the business could plan accordingly. In so doing, we would know the best point to introduce occupational health to assist with people's recovery and planned return to work.

"You must also ring me every fuckin' day whilst you are off and give me an update on your progress. Some of you will return to work as quickly as you can. Others among you are lazy little bastards who will string it out for as long as possible. So, pick up that dog and bone and talk to me. I'm a reasonable man, I'll understand if you have flu, but if you have a sniffling little cold and are being a right pussy about coming back to work then we'll have a different kind of chat. Comprende?"

We introduced early intervention by Occupational Health when it looked like someone would be off for longer than a week. We trained line managers and team leaders about the importance of welfare and well-being; making sure that people were fit to return to work. Graduated returns from long term absence and light duties were encouraged for set periods. People could adjust, especially when they were recovering from injuries. Some managers understood this welfare-driven approach more than others.

"As far as I'm concerned lad, if you walk through that door, you're declaring yourself fit for work. If you're not, then don't fuckin' bother. I can't have someone employed to lug boxes and cages around if they can't lug fuckin' boxes and cages around, know what I mean?"

We asked managers to look at the number of days absence that people had taken over a rolling twelve-month period. If there had been a pattern of odd days off, or every Tuesday following a bank holiday Monday, then this should be addressed in a return to work interview. Similarly, if there was a recurrence of absences with one underlying cause, such as a bad back, this was a trigger to involve occupational health. They might, in turn, arrange for physiotherapy for the affected employee. Then again, some managers were more empathetic than others.

"Let's face it, lad, you've had more snotty noses than Quinn the fuckin' Eskimo, so I suggest you neck some paracetamol, bring a packet of Lockets to work and belt the fuck up!"

As a last resort, the company would take disciplinary action against repeat offenders who were not fulfilling their contracts of employment. Some of the tougher management decisions were fully justified, whereas others required a little more compassion. It was my role to monitor the absence levels, support line managers, stay in touch with employees who were 'long term absentees', give direction about pay and oversee some potentially awkward conversations, guiding them to the right conclusion.

The reasons that employees gave for their absences were many and varied. I sometimes wondered if people made it up or tried to outdo each other for a laugh, but, where warranted, I had to remain straight-faced, pragmatic and concerned.

Phil, for example, was off work with a bad back and had been for some time. Imagine our surprise when it came to light that he was doing a sponsored parachute jump at Morecambe Bay. But imagine Phil's ultimate surprise when Tom ('I need to see this with my own bloody eyes, Gemma!'), John and I were there to greet him upon his landing back down to earth with a big bump. His immediate response was to ask his union rep how on earth he was going to get him out of this sticky situation. Alex's conclusion? 'You're going to need Perry Mason to get you out of this one, son!'

Then there was Kevin, a Jack-the-Lad warehouse operative who, at the last count, had nine Grandmas who had sadly 'passed away' in the space of six months. Either this was an extreme case of the modern 'blended family' or a loophole in the system. Authorised 'bereavement leave' to attend the funeral of a loved one didn't count as an absence in terms of your overall attendance record. Kevin may have got away with four or five, but he had been royally taking the Schmeichel.

The people who were most honest about their reasons for absence were my absolute favourites. I often felt that they would be better off fibbing about it. I almost felt bad holding them to task for their absence records when they presented the most compelling cases for needing to be away from work. Over the months and years, there was a steady procession of people through the door and some of my favourite encounters from the subsequent return to work interviews and investigations with line managers were as follows:

1. *The 'not so lucky' lotto numbers*

Me: 'So tell us why you didn't make it to work last Monday?'

Lindsay (sniffing back tears slightly): 'I honestly thought I'd won the lottery. But I bloody hadn't had I?!'

Me: 'Well, I'm sorry to hear that. It must have come as a shock. How did you come to be so confused?'

Lindsay: 'I was pissed as a fart when the results came in. I didn't check the numbers until after my shift had finished the next day. I'm a massive tit and I'm sorry. Can I have my job back now?'

Me: 'I'm sure we can look at that, but you might want to apologise to John for leaving a message on his answering machine telling him and I quote, that 'he can shove his shitty job up his shitty fucking arse.'

Lindsay (still sniffling): 'Aye alright. Course, I will.'

2. *The Long Lunch*

Me (on the phone): 'Hi Laurie, it's Gemma from HR at work. Just checking everything's ok because you haven't come back to work after lunch today. Is everything alright?'

Laurie: 'Shit! I forgot! Thought it was the end of the day, I'm just sat at home watching Neighbours - I thought it was the tea-time episode!!'

3. *Blessed Billy*

Me: 'How you doing Billy? I noticed you didn't make it in yesterday. Is everything ok with you?'

Billy: 'I got lucky on Wednesday night. Woke up and didn't have a fucking clue where I was. Took me 'til lunchtime to find a road sign and hitch back from Widnes.'

Me: 'Right. Well, happens to us all I guess.' Not.

4. *Front of House Freda (who sometimes covered for Sandra on Reception)*

Me (on the phone): 'Morning Freda, it's Gemma calling from work, just wondering if everything's ok because you're not in as yet and there's no one on the switchboard. I wasn't sure if you'd been trying to call or not. Are you ok?'

Freda: 'Fine thanks, love. It's just that my hair's

still green from that Halloween Party I went to on Saturday and I didn't think it would go with the colour scheme in reception.'

Me: 'Ok. And you didn't think to let us know?'

Freda: 'Well, I couldn't get through, could I?' with a cackling laugh.

5. *Life's a Beach*

Paul Tetley: 'Where the fuck were you yesterday?'

Terrorised employee: 'Erm well, my doctor said I had a Vitamin D deficiency, so I decided to take the family to Southport Beach for the day.'

Paul Tetley: 'You fuckin' what?!'

6. *Marital Bliss*

Frank (on the Warehouse answer machine, speaking nervously and sheepishly): 'Hello. It's Frank from D Shift. Erm sorry I've left it a bit late, I know I'm meant to be in work in 20 minutes but erm the thing is that I forgot I was doing something quite important today. I forgot until just now when my fiancée reminded me with a kick to the knackers. I'm in a bit of bother, to be honest, but the thing is I completely forgot that I'm getting married today.'

Poor Frank. Poor Frank's Missus. Poor knackers!

7. *Family Ties*

Me: 'So, I'm afraid we cannot allow your request to take a day's paid bereavement leave for your girlfriend's rabbit's funeral. If you'd like to take a

HAVE YOU GOT A MINUTE?

holiday, so that you can have the time with her, it wouldn't be a problem?'

Jerry: 'That is so unfair!'

Me: 'Help me to understand why it's unfair.'

Jerry: 'It's unfair because I was step-dad to that rabbit and I have been asked by my loved one to be a pallbearer at the funeral, which is a *very* important role. I thought people in HR were meant to be sympathetic? Surely means I should get two days paid bereavement leave, never mind one!'

Me: 'I'm not sure there's much else to discuss here, let me know if you'd like the day off as holiday and I'll put it through for you.'

Jerry (shaking his fist at me): 'I'm going to write to my MP about this. It's about animal rights as well as human ones. I think there will be great media interest in this!'

Alex, the trusty union rep: 'Don't be a wanker. Come on; we're off.'

8. *Vanity Rules*

Tony Slater: 'I can't come in today Tom. Got a dicky tummy.'

Tom: 'Bullshit, man. What's happened?'

Tony Slater: 'I was dying my eyebrows and some 'Just for Men' ran into my right eye. I can see fuck all. My eyeball is scorched!'

Tom: 'Bloody hell, Tony!'

9. *Love Letters Straight from Her Majesty's*

143

Prison (on prison stamped writing paper)

'Dear Gemma,

Sorry I haven't been in touch for a while or been in work. As you might be aware, I've been unavoidably detained at Her Majesty's pleasure for the foreseeable future.

But if you could see your way to keeping my job open and asking Frank on D shift to do my lottery whilst I'm away I'd be very grateful.

Yours in hope,

Harry Price

I'd become aware of Harry's misfortune as his case appeared in the local papers. The outcome of his trial had unfolded before my very eyes on Look North the night before. He'd punched someone repeatedly outside a nightclub and, whilst that person had provoked Harry, the victim had suffered life-changing injuries. Nice that Harry was in a position to think about life after his release date though and the all-important lottery syndicate.

Sticking with the prison theme, we had a pregnant employee whose boyfriend had been told to expect a lengthy prison term for importing and selling Class A drugs. Unfortunately for Denise, he lived with her and she was also expecting a prison sentence for aiding and abetting. She had known what he was doing as he was temporarily storing the stolen goods in her attic, essentially running a mini Harfield operation from their home in Chadderton.

To be fair, she did come to me and tell me

everything before her sentencing took place. Denise was usually a confident, outgoing, borderline cocky character. She was very outspoken and could be quite tricky to manage. But I could tell Denise was scared. She had a five-year-old daughter called Destiny. Denise was worried about what would happen to her. She was also concerned about what would happen to her new-born baby, fathered by Leigh's answer to Pablo Escobar. Of course, the child would be born in prison and she wanted to know if she would have a job at the end of the sentence. Denise asked if we could write a letter detailing her usually good disposition, loyal service and ask for leniency as recent events were entirely out of character. I wasn't sure that I could stretch it quite that far but assured her that we would come up with something; we were well used to writing letters for our employees to use in court but usually for speeding offences rather than drug trafficking. As long as Harfield Distribution's name was kept out of the media, there was generally room for a discussion about helping employees. I would need to be creative in this case because Jenny was not the model employee and we weren't sure we wanted her back after she had served her time.

We had a general rule of thumb that we would look at each case on its own merits and consider any mitigating factors. If employees were sentenced to long prison terms, it wasn't reasonable or expected that we would keep their job open. In employment law terms, the relationship between long prison sentences and employment was known as 'frustration of contract', which effectively ended the mutual obligation to provide work and provide services. However, Denise was pregnant and this was a definite curveball in that well-tested theory.

Tom, John and Tony were reluctant to give her any assurances about her job. It was down to me to break the news to them that it would largely depend on the length of her sentence. At that time, paternity leave wasn't available, but female employees would receive six months of statutory maternity pay and then could take an additional three months off work unpaid. In theory, if Denise's custodial sentence was the same or less than this period, she could argue that we'd have to keep her job open anyway. It was just the little matter of prison that was an inconvenient truth when looking at the time off she was entitled to take.

"That's bloody ridiculous!" protested Tom.

"I know, but it's the law." I countered. "If she's going to be off work anyway on maternity leave, she can bring a claim if we don't treat her fairly in the eyes of employment law."

"That's bloody ridiculous!" repeated Tom, uncharacteristically lost for other expletives.

"Let's just see what happens and take it from there - it might just resolve itself, depending on how long she gets," was the best assurance I could offer at this stage.

HAVE YOU GOT A MINUTE?

As it happened, Denise was sentenced to two years imprisonment with the potential to be released after one year for good behaviour. She gave birth to her son, Rambo (naturally) in Her Majesty's Prison Styal. She was unable to maintain any good behaviour so ended up serving the full sentence and more for other misdemeanours committed inside. As far as I knew, her daughter went to live with Denise's mum and her son remained in prison with her for the first eighteen months of his life. I wasn't sure what happened after that, because we didn't keep in touch, but I heard on the grapevine that the kids would be raised together in any case.

In work, we were stepping up our efforts to be more 'on it' regarding absence management. Jan was overseeing this across all her sites and was able to share best practice that she'd gathered from other HR Directors on different Harfield Distribution contracts. Our warehouse manager, John, took his new responsibility as a member of the 'absence police' very seriously. So much so that upon finding out that one of his warehouse operatives was off, with a by all accounts nasty stomach bug, he could not rest until he had made a phone call to cajole him back into work.

"Steven, get yourself back into work lad, it can't be that bad!"

"But John, I'm constantly rushing to the toilet and I'd be worried about handling food in this state. There's no chance I can get in."

"Steven lad, the simple fact is that we've got more toilets here than you've got at home. You can shit yourself silly then wash your hands in nice hot soapy water! Get yourself in!"

I was with Steven, on this occasion, but was pleased with John's level of commitment to the cause. Continuing his drive to raise standards, our John was even more determined to tackle the erratic attendance patterns of Kate and Ruth. They were a lesbian couple, in a loving relationship, who both worked in the warehouse. They were either both in work together or both off work together. One did not appear without the other which was a mightily frustrating double whammy when orders had to be picked, packed and shipped on time, every time.

Synchronised menstrual cycles had rendered them incapable of both coming into work at key points in the month. The main query here was the fact that according to HR and occupational health records, Kate and Ruth had both had hysterectomies and full removal of ovaries some time ago. Yet, ten years later, here they were both off work with period pains, despite not having a set of ovaries between them. Before confronting them, John tried to make sense of the situation with me, but in all honesty, it blew his mind. As every schoolgirl knows, you only have to mention 'monthlies', 'lady bits' or 'the blob' to a man in authority, for them to run a million miles away. The girls wasted no time dropping similar words into the conversation.

"I know it might seem strange, but we can't help it if our wombs are totally…" started Kate.

"In sync," finished Ruth.

"Our bodies still think there's a ruby-red egg…" continued Kate.

"Ready to drop every month into our gusset," replied Ruth.

And the icing on the cake: "To be quite frank, John," began Kate.

"It can often look like a butcher's bin downstairs and we don't want to bring that to work with us," concluded Ruth.

By this time, John was stuffing his fist into his mouth and looking anywhere but at the girls. Time to intervene. Kate and Ruth's claims of 'ghost period pain' following the latest absences just wouldn't cut it with me. It was up to me to guide John through the appropriate conversation. I suggested explaining that whilst we were not medical experts, the scenario presented seemed unlikely and the simple fact was, they were not meeting the requirements of their contract of employment, i.e. turning up and putting in a shift. John made detailed notes of the conversation as I spoke to the ladies, making sure that our message was clear and understood.

Furthermore, we needed them to fully comprehend our expectation that the other person must come to work when the other one was ill and vice versa, which seemed to come as a surprise to them. Once John had composed himself and after a short adjournment, I advised him to listen to any counterarguments or mitigating circumstances that the girls might have. He was to ask appropriate questions and not pre-judge anything but also be firm and fair when delivering expectations.

The meeting re-started well and as far as Ruth and Kate were concerned, they saw nothing wrong with taking time off together.

"We're a..." started Kate.

"Team," finished Ruth.

"I don't want to be in work…" commenced Kate.

"... without her," concluded Ruth.

Sweet sentiments, but they didn't help John to run his warehouse operation effectively with two people down at the same time every month. After more conversation, John was ready to conclude.

"Look ladies, I'm no Claire Rayner, (TV agony aunt for decades, in case you were wondering), but even I know that you can't have that kind of pain when all of your equipment has been removed. You are properly taking the piss here and you need to leave your period dramas at home."

Just to add insult to injury for John, the pinnacle of their audacity came when Kate and Ruth requested maternity leave when their beloved Labrador, Princess Pocahontas Paula Janice Juniper Wright, came to have puppies. Further to a litany of incredulous expletives, their request was swiftly rejected by John. So, they put in a grievance, 'heartbroken and devastated' that their 'perfectly

HAVE YOU GOT A MINUTE?

reasonable request' had been so cruelly denied. They argued that they had been 'discriminated against'. They regarded the event as the closest they would get to be parents or grandparents and they felt that their sexuality was the reason for the rejected request.

Unfortunately for them, Paul Tetley was assigned to hear their grievance. John couldn't do it, as the complaint was against him and Tony didn't want to know. After giving the girls a full twenty-five seconds to explain their concerns, Paul was ready to wrap up.

"Listen, girls. I just want to assure you that your sexuality has sweet fuck all to do with rejecting your request for maternity leave. You can fiddle with each other's fannies all day long as far as I'm concerned." I flashed him a look and he quickly coughed and returned to point.

"Your request has been rejected because you're not entitled to maternity leave when your dog has puppies. Frankly, it's a shite request and therefore your grievance will not be upheld. So, get yourselves back to work and move on. I can tell you're upset, so feel free to comfort each other. Maybe hug, give each other a little kiss or a cuddle that's it, a little hug goes a long way!" Horrified to have witnessed another tutorial in how to navigate the world through the eyes of Paul Tetley, I gently ushered him out of the room, ready to engage in another diplomacy talk. You'll not be surprised to hear that my comment to Paul that he was 'such a cliché' was utterly lost on him.

Grievance wise, that was that. Thankfully, Ruth and Kate had left the room before Paul turned and addressed me.

"There's no way I could have agreed to that, or we'd have every Emma and Gemma coming to us for time off when their pets give birth. Beyond a joke that! Pissing ridiculous!"

Political correctness was not on Paul's radar. I don't think he even had a radar. I was, however, temporarily buoyed by the fact that at least he knew not to say certain things in front of them and that he had the good grace to wait until Ruth and Kate had left the room.

Paul's new-found tact and diplomacy didn't last long. My temporary illusions were shattered pretty quickly when we met with the lovely Valerie Drocher, a reliable, conscientious customer liaison specialist. Following a recent cancer scare after a routine smear test, she dutifully informed the company that she would need to have a sustained absence from work for major abdominal surgery - a full hysterectomy to be exact. Thankfully, the operation went well. At Valerie's welfare check, which took place before her phased return to work, Paul Tetley took heed of Tom's instruction to establish the finer details of the absence. He asked her to explain in detail exactly what a 'hist-o-rectumy' was ('hysterectomy' in the language of Wigan). Despite my trying to kerb this line of enquiry, Paul was on a roll. He continued to interrogate Valerie about wombs, ovaries and fallopian tubes in a level of detail that would impress Sir Robert Winston. I was wincing on behalf of Valerie, but she didn't seem to mind educating Paul at all and articulated her answers very well.

After a pause and my great relief that Paul had exhausted his line of questioning, he opened his mouth one last time to summarise just how he saw things.

"So... basically love, what you're saying is that your nursery is still open, but your playpen's fucked?"

Valerie had no answer to that and neither did I. I snapped my notebook shut, thanked her for coming in and escorted her back to reception, glaring at a very amused Paul throughout.

I made a mental note to arrange some 'absence handling' training for managers and guidance on having difficult conversations. This would include examples of what was appropriate to say or ask in the workplace and what wasn't; how to manage people and situations with respect, dignity and compassion; understanding when to speak and when not to speak. Period.

Chapter 10

YOU NEVER GET A SECOND CHANCE TO MAKE A FIRST IMPRESSION

Recruitment was a continuous process in all of the distribution centres and across most departments. We were still in the era of pre-automation and relied heavily on people-power to support labour-intensive processes. As demands from the customer fluctuated, so did our headcount requirements. Sometimes this meant having to get creative when we needed to increase numbers at short notice.

"Gemma!" Tom would holler as he burst into my office, not bothering to check who was there, or whether they might have been in tears in the middle of a conversation, or not. "I need forty more people to pick and pack starting next Tuesday for six weeks. I don't care how you get 'em, but as long as they can read, tell the difference between milk and sprouts and have a pulse, they'll probably do for us."

High standards indeed were set.

We liaised heavily with temporary-worker agencies, creating a 'managed service' approach that allowed us ongoing access to a pool of trained people. In addition to this, in a moment of brilliance, warehouse manager, John shared more pearls of his infinite wisdom.

"I think we should advertise in different languages given the location of the sites and the different nationalities that live in the surrounding areas. We live in a culturally rich, diverse country, you know. I heard John Prescott say so on the news and if that numb nut's noticed, then it must be true."

Our sites were all over the country, but the main ones I looked after were in the north and north west of England on industrial estates on the outskirts of inner cities. To be fair to John, his idea wasn't a bad shout. Tom was willing to try anything and the other senior managers were on-board pretty quickly. Only things did not run smoothly or go according to any form of plan. There were a couple of flaws in John's thought process. None of the management team were of ethnic origin or came from outside of the Lancashire-Merseyside border; Halifax was considered to be a foreign country for most of them. We were unable to check the content of a translated job advert. When I suggested that we employ the services of a translation agency to make sure our market-facing material was linguistically correct, Tom promptly told me that we didn't have money to burn. Instead, we decided to ask a few employees to help us out. The reliable ones, who we knew would do a conscientious job, like Abdul in the Warehouse. He was a good lad, team leader material and we knew that he'd do his best. What we didn't realise was that his spoken English was better than his grasp of written Urdu which, as it turned, out mainly consisted of colloquial family cuss words. So, when Abdul diligently translated our advert, it should have read something like:

New Vacancies at Harfield Distribution

Are you looking for a new challenge? Would you like to contribute to the success of Britain's leading supermarket chain? If so, then we would love to hear from you.

Harfield Distribution is hiring warehouse operatives, drivers and administrative employees to join their teams in Haydock and Leigh. We'd love to talk to you about joining our team.

We can offer a range of different shift patterns, job security, career progression opportunities and NVQs for those who wish to undertake them. You'll be joining a well-established, rapidly expanding team who will show you the ropes; full training will be provided and the pay is competitive.

In return, we're looking for hard-working, diligent people who have excellent attention to detail.

Interested parties should send a letter of application and CV to Gemma Walters, HR Officer, Harfield Logistics, Brownberry Lane, Haydock Industrial Estate.

Unfortunately, it read more like:

New Vacancies at Harfield Distribution

You want new job? Wanna work at Pricetown?

Harfield Distribution are hiring people, but only clever ones. Don't want no donkeys. Only incompetent people should apply. You can work in warehouse, admin or drive a massive truck.

Shift patterns can be hardcore, but on earlies, you can pick the kids up, on lates you can have a lie-in before work, watch Prisoner Cell Block H to wind down and on nights... well there ain't no upside to nights really. You're always banjaxed.

The job will be there long time. You can even get some exams n' shit. People will show you what to do but watch out coz there's some right jokers.

Most intelligent applicants are welcome, but may God take your soul if you are not capable. Only serious people please, nothing stinky, no time wasters and no pimps.

Interested parties should send a letter of application and CV to Gemma Walters, HR Officer, Harfield Logistics, Brownberry Lane, Haydock Industrial Estate.

Our success in this particular campaign was limited. It generated a lot of interest but not necessarily for the right reasons. I'll always be grateful and simultaneously horrified when thinking of the member of the public who called to let us know the nature of our advertising. Time to let Tom know where his frugality had landed us.

Our second attempt, after paying for a translator (after several exclamations of 'bloody hell!' from Tom) to screen the adverts, help interview and recruit several candidates, the second flaw in John's plan came to light at a most inopportune time. We were showing Pricetown around the shop floor during one of their regular site visits. The goal was to showcase our ingenuity and introduce them to some of our new employees. Only, when we got to the shop floor, the recruits weren't exactly what I'd call a hive of activity. They were standing in a cluster around the drinks machine with puzzled looks on their faces, a collection of what seemed like permanently furrowed brows. As it turned out, I couldn't blame them. It was all very well advertising in foreign languages; it was even better recruiting a good number of people to start during a time of peak production - we were very proud of ourselves. Only, there wasn't too much to brag about when the customer asked how the bloody hell they were meant to pick and pack products when the bloody work tickets were printed in plain bloody English and not bloody Urdu. That would explain the clusters of recruits hanging around and waiting for direction.

And, just like that, we started all over again with our recruitment campaign. John had his tail between his legs once more and we all felt like complete losers. Not one of us had thought to check stage two of the brilliant brainwave until it was way too late. That said, Pricetown did seriously look into printing work tickets in different languages because they could see the merits of the idea. Unfortunately, it was shelved before it began as it would have been a hugely expensive, cost-prohibitive project.

Everyone who did make it through the stringent recruitment process was given a twelve-week probationary period and, after this, we decided whether or not to offer them a permanent position. The terms were pretty ruthless in making sure that the right people were hired. One absence, one late mark, one missed shift, one misjudged comment and they would be yesterday's news, even when English was barely a second language.

Some of the hiring managers took a rather arrogant view of their workforce. They felt that local people should feel incredibly honoured to work early shifts (6.00 a.m. – 2.00 p.m.); late shifts (2.00 p.m. – 10.00 p.m.) and night shifts (10.00 p.m. – 6.00 a.m.); all for a minimum wage (not *the* minimum wage - this was still being discussed in Parliament and wasn't yet a legal requirement). I worked hard to instil the view that recruitment is a two-way process and we as a company should be promoting the benefits of working for the country's largest supermarket and the career opportunities we could offer. Of course, we wanted to secure the best people for the job, but we also had to 'sell the dream' of working for our business to the candidates. To be fair, what we could offer them in terms of stability, career progression and a healthy dose of overtime to supplement their income did outweigh a lot of our competitors on the same industrial estates. These things made it a more straightforward process in a lot of respects. On the flipside, convincing my colleagues that recruitment and on-boarding was a reciprocal arrangement between employer and employee was not a view that everyone shared.

"Bollocks. Do they want a pissin' job or not?" said Paul Tetley initially.

"We have to be honest about the job, the hard graft and the shift patterns, but try to sell it to them as well. We offer a lot and we should stick by what we say in the interview once they start or we'll risk losing them to Jenner's down the road; we only pay 5p an hour more than them, so we have to try and stand out. Be the employer of choice." I countered.

"Choice? They can choose to fuckin' work here, or they can choose to piss off somewhere else. It's not rocket science." Right. I noted that some 'Recruitment Refresher' workshops might be required.

I had my work cut out. Reminding managers to be enthusiastic in interviews was tricky.

"They should be grateful we're even seeing them!" snorted Tony Slater. His hair was jet black on this occasion - freshly topped up ahead of the interviews.

"Wrong, Tony. Interviewing is a two-way process and the candidates are interested in us as much as we are them. Our job is to convince them that working here is more stable, more secure and offers more opportunity than somewhere else around the corner. Everyone is advertising; everyone is hiring, it's a candidate's market in these parts, so we need to stand out and show why we're different or, at least a more attractive prospect than other businesses in the vicinity." I was doing my best here!

"Right. Ok. I think I've got it. A squirt of Brut should do it. The lady candidates will like that. Never fails to make me a more attractive prospect," he offered, whilst licking his palms and then smoothing down his sideburns. Tony was clearly missing the point here, but I suspected that he was a lost cause.

Keeping managers on the right side of employment law, whilst recruiting, wasn't always easy either. Whilst 'hiring managers' couldn't exactly do or say what they liked (there was some legislation and there were specific rules) the training had been minimal. Here we were before the 'Equality Act', which didn't come into force until 2010. We had things like the 'Disability Discrimination Act' and the 'Sex Discrimination Act', but nothing as comprehensive and all-encompassing as the 'Equality Act', which eventually became statute. To be candid, people got away with a lot more then than they should or could now, but there were still rules.

To help understand where we were with this and build my own understanding of the business further,

I decided to sit in with the hiring managers when they were interviewing. In doing so, I boosted my own learning about the various departments on-site and helped find out how the business was being 'sold' to prospective employees. Plus, I hoped it showed the managers that HR cared and wanted the best for the company. Most of the interviews went well and attracted a good number of quality candidates. But some of the questions asked by hiring managers were simply outrageous. Some of them that caused my blood pressure to rise included:

'Are you married? Any plans for kids soon?' (Women only).

'What religion are you, lad? We don't have a prayer room here.' (To no one of Caucasian appearance).

'Will you be able to lug that pallet around if you're fasting?' (Only to Asian candidates, regardless of actual religion).

And for the avoidance of doubt, the idea of giving people a chance to rehabilitate after prison or that a 'spent' conviction meant they had served their time was non-existent.

'If you've got a criminal record, you're not coming in. I don't give a frog's fat arse about how sorry you are or that you're more of a reformed character than Dr fuckin' Doom, you're not setting a foot through this door!'

Not surprisingly, Paul Tetley demonstrated a wealth of experience when it came to inappropriate questions. I had been sitting in on an interview with a young woman who was a perfect fit for the transport scheduler role on offer. Just as the interview was drawing to a close, the candidate having conducted herself with the utmost professionalism, Paul Tetley proclaimed, "Just one more from me lass. How old are you and have you been spayed?"

Gobsmacked (again!), I jumped in with, "Really sorry about that; it's just his left-field sense of humour, he didn't mean it at all. Thank you so much for your time today and we'll be in touch very soon."

The candidate nodded awkwardly and said her goodbyes. Failing to follow our own home-grown mantra of 'always let the candidates know the outcome', we never did get in touch... but thankfully neither did she - with a lawsuit!

It was time for some intervention.

Jan and I pulled together a workshop on recruitment for hiring managers. We covered best practice and the full recruitment cycle from advertising, to creating job descriptions, the various recruitment processes at our disposal and onboarding. Most importantly, we trained the managers on the basics of employment law, arming them with appropriate questions they could ask and being abundantly clear about the type of questions that they should not.

Underneath the bluster, Paul was a bright man and he knew what he was doing. He understood the importance of doing things in the right way, but he continued to make outrageous comments wherever he could and, whilst very amusing, they could have landed us in hot water all too easily. Jan decided it was time for some revenge, considering how much backtracking and intervention we had to do to save the business from one of Paul's classic comments. A plan was hatched.

He was advertising for an Admin Assistant in the Transport Department and we'd had a decent response to the advert. According to Paul, there wasn't anyone suitable internally; no one quite hit the right credentials. When Derek from the Warehouse applied, for example, he bluntly declared that the role was 'women's work', knowing full well that he couldn't say that at all. So, Jan and I worked on a fake CV from a candidate called Vanessa Snowball and made sure it ticked all the boxes in terms of the person spec, job description and advert. Paul wouldn't be able to turn this candidate away for an interview, that was for sure.

We brought Tom in on the act and arranged a recruitment review meeting so that we could update Tom on all the open positions and how far we were in the process with each vacancy. When it came to the Transport Department, we were able to show that we'd had a good response and had whittled down the CV's to three for interview.

"This Vanessa Snowball looks promising," said Tom. "Seems to have all the right credentials and experience."

"Yes," agreed Paul, "Stupid name but she does look good on paper. Hope she looks as fit in real life as she does in black and white!" he said, winking at me.

I rolled my eyes in mock disgust and asked, "Have you thought about where you might interview her?"

"How do you mean? I'll just do it in my office like always," he said.

"Well, that might be difficult given that she's in a wheelchair," said Jan, deadpan. "She'll never make it up the stairs to your office and the modifications we're making to the downstairs meeting rooms and elevators won't be ready for a few weeks yet."

"Right. Well, not sure then. Where do you think would be suitable?" Paul asked, already shifting awkwardly in his seat.

"Well, we could explain to her that we're having work done to be able to access the building more easily, but it isn't ready yet. Given that we're keen to see her, we could offer to meet her somewhere neutral with wheelchair access and give her the option of where. She might have some recommendations and be more clued up than us on where is best around here," I said.

"Yep, that sounds alreet. Will you talk to her and let me know where and when?" Paul asked.

"Course. No problem," I said.

Paul made a move to stand and go back to work. "And don't forget about the translator," said Jan casually, not looking up from her papers.

"Translator," said Paul incredulously. "Where's she from?"

"Uganda," said Jan. "She's asked that we organise a translator and pay for it for the interview, although her written English is very good."

"You fuckin' what? Paying for translators? How's she gonna do the job if she needs a translator?"

"Well, this is what we need to establish Paul," said Tom casually.

"Nothing is too much trouble for the right candidate."

"Fuck me. You've changed!" said Paul mockingly.

"I guess the translator might also be Vanessa's guide." I chipped in.

"Guide?" asked Paul, now perspiring slightly.

"Yes. It says on her Equal Ops form that she's partially sighted. We might arrange the interview verbally, by telephone, but I'm looking into braille options in the interests of covering all bases." I said, biting the inside of my cheek, so I didn't give anything away.

"Hang on a bloody minute. You're saying I need to interview someone off-site who is blind, in a wheelchair and doesn't speak a word of the Queen's?" He was bordering on incandescent by this point.

"Well, it's important not to pre-judge Paul. She has an excellent CV," said Jan.

"For fuck's sake!" muttered Paul. "Let's get on

with it then."

"One more thing," said Jan, before he left, "Vanessa is in the same-sex partnership with her partner Namazzi, a campaigner for race equality in the UK. Please be aware of this and be careful when you're interviewing her. It's a claim waiting to happen, so I'm asking Gemma to meet her with you and do most of the talking, ok?"

"Christ on a bike!" said Paul. "It probably makes sense that Gemma does that, but the whole thing sounds like a fuckin' nightmare to be honest."

"Now, now Paul," chided Tom softly. "I know it seems complex, but we just have to be open, honest and mindful that the girl's CV is excellent and she might do a crackin' job for us. The rest is just noise - if she can do the job, we'll figure everything else out."

"Whatever you say, Tom," said Paul, gobsmacked and worried about having to be on best behaviour.

For the next few days, I told Paul that the interview had been arranged and that we would be meeting Vanessa at a local pub famous for weekend carveries but open for coffee and drinks in the week. We agreed that I would drive and when he called in my office to set off, Jan, Tom and I greeted him with a great big 'Gotcha!!'

"You bastards!" said Paul once we'd told him the whole thing was a hoax. "I've been shittin' bricks all week." He was smiling, though.

"Good!" said Jan laughing. "That was the

intention!"

It was naughty of us, really - political correctness was utterly out of the window. However, I think Paul got the point that his throwaway comments were not appropriate or fair and that he was probably dismissing some candidates based on his prejudices. It didn't stop him entirely, of course, but just being able to say 'remember Vanessa Snowball' with a wry look was enough to make him backtrack and reconsider his words.

In other circumstances and on occasions, candidates didn't exactly help themselves. I've seen plenty of them turn up late, drunk, smoking, tripping, stoned, asleep whilst waiting to be called in and others chewing gum like a cow chomping cud throughout the interview. Even more baffling is when I've seen people spitting outside reception in a pre-interview ritual, often dressed like young offenders on day release rather than for a prospective new position. I don't mind what people wear for job interviews as long as it's clean and job appropriate. When it's an all grey Reebok tracksuit with a week's worth of unmentionable stains and blood splatters, it does create a certain sense of what we might expect should the candidate be successful. However, we always gave people a chance and we're happy to be proven wrong at the first impression stage.

The second impression is a different prospect altogether. Especially when a candidate hasn't been successful in progressing to the next stage in the process and their mother rings the HR Department to find out why or writes an eight-page hand-written letter to find out why little Arnold hasn't got the job. Little Arnold is typically around the age of forty-eight and living in the box room at his mum's house. He's usually really bright, been in the same job somewhere else since school and likes to dress in hand-knitted tank tops, full suit, shirt and tie on hot summer days. Nothing wrong with that as such, but unfortunately, little Arnold has usually been so cossetted that he has very few social skills and would be eaten alive in a robust environment such as one of Harfield's Distribution warehouses. I am amazed how often the parents of grown people see fit to interfere with their offspring's career path. I can understand it for school leavers, graduates or young people starting in their first role. We would often host open days and welcome meetings for this very purpose, inviting families along to look around the operation, but where the recruits are closer to forty or fifty in age, it's a bit odd.

Depending on the vacancy we were hiring for, we occasionally asked candidates to prepare presentations. Sometimes we gave them a specific topic to speak on for five to ten minutes, relevant to the role to which they were applying. Other times, we would let them pick a topic of their own, especially if the aim was to test their presenting skills rather than the content of their speech. A few of the managers and I would form a panel and take turns to ask candidates questions about their presentation. One particular candidate, who had applied for a team leader position in the warehouse, was tasked with speaking for five minutes on any subject of his choice, be it personal or professional. We told him we were looking at his presenting style rather than the content and focusing accordingly. Most people chose a hobby to talk about or something relevant to their job or the prospective role. Maybe we should have been more specific with this guy because he seemed to think it was perfectly normal to go into great detail about the digestive system (unusual but ok); bowel movements (less ok); colonic content (bordering on odd) and a full-blown account about the various types of faeces that humans could produce (straight-up weird).

At the end of a tortuous five minutes for all concerned, warehouse manager Tony shuffled uncomfortably in his chair, scratching his 'light brown with hints of summer' barnet.

Tony's colleague John chipped in, "Well that was different, lad!"

Liz was laughing her head off uncontrollably, giving the occasional snort and couldn't pull it together at all.

Paul Tetley declared unequivocally, "What a load of old shite!!" which for once was both accurate *and* appropriate.

By the end of the cursed presentation, we were all rolling in the aisles, tears streaming down our faces.

It was possibly the most unprofessional moment in my career to date, but the more we tried not to laugh, the more we guffawed - like when you're laughing in assembly at school and desperately trying to hold it in but failing. Suffice to say, this poor chap didn't get the job and I had some work to do to apologise for our collective immaturity, whilst trying to weave it into some constructive feedback.

Further to this, our prank on Paul and a litany of disastrous recruitment campaigns, Jan and I set about designing a process map for recruitment. We pulled together a workshop to go through it with hiring managers. We covered best practice examples from UK industry and the full recruitment cycle from advertising to creating job descriptions, the various recruitment processes at our disposal and onboarding once people started work with us - often a forgotten thing. Most importantly, we trained the managers about the basics of employment law. Most of the managers understood and bought into this systemised, open and fair way of recruiting that kept them on the right side of the law. The process was lost entirely on others, but at least we could demonstrate that we had delivered appropriate training.

For a while there were no more recruitment-related incidents. I think we made progress as the morally reprehensible/illegal questions disappeared from the typical rhetoric that had been present beforehand. That said, you can't account for everything through a series of crystal-clear training programmes and constant reminders to managers - no siree!

Such an example was eminently demonstrated in an interview with a lovely candidate by the name of Sarah Bond. She had applied for the position as Admin Assistant in the Transport Department, following Vanessa Snowball's no-show at interview. Funny that. I'd given Paul the hard word before we went in. I reminded him of the training that he'd recently undertaken and the framed certificate that was proudly hanging in his office to prove it (and which might prove helpful if, or indeed, when we were sued for something he'd said or done). I also revisited the importance of creating a good impression and how it was his job to make sure the candidate had a positive experience and left the building feeling buoyed, whatever the eventual outcome might be.

"Is she fit?" he asked just as we were about to go in. I glared at him as he grinned at me and said, "What did I say?"

The interview went well, which was something of a relief. Sarah had a solid, proven track record in admin and had worked in similar environments to ours. She seemed well used to the fast pace of life that we'd all come to know and love. In short, she was perfect for the job. We concluded the interview and said we would be in touch as soon as possible, strongly hinting that a second stage interview was on the cards. We explained to Sarah that she might meet prospective colleagues and some of the other managers in the business at this point. She seemed excited by this and told us of her availability for an interview over the next couple of weeks. Sarah said she liked the sound of the role and the business and would like to meet us again soon. As we wrapped up proceedings, I opened the door and led her back to reception, where she would exit the building and go about her business... or so I had thought.

"What did you think?" I asked Paul as I popped back into the interview room.

"Yep, good, not bad," he said, which was enthusiastic praise indeed from him!

"I think she'd be a perfect fit. She'd get on with the team well and I think she'd pick up the work pretty quickly because of her background in warehousing," I enthused. "I think she'd be really good for us."

"Mmm..." said Paul, absent-mindedly. I sensed that something wasn't quite right and that he could be having second thoughts.

"What is it? Do you have any doubts?" I asked nervously.

"No, no, I think she's alright," he said.

"Then what is it? Something's bothering you..." I wish I'd never asked.

"Well, she's a nice woman and seems very capable. She'd probably do an alright job. It's just that, well if I were that fuckin' ugly I'd probably shave my arse and walk on my hands," he concluded.

Another 'wow' moment that would have otherwise been fine, if only Sarah hadn't forgotten to take her scarf when she left and popped back through to the interview room to get it, hearing everything he'd said. We all just looked at each other awkwardly. I started to mumble apologies, but a tearful Sarah simply walked out of the door in an understandable flap.

Thinking that Paul might be mortified or at least show a modicum of remorse I gave him my best 'what the fuck…?' quizzical mum look, hoping for some kind of reaction.

"How would you feel if someone spoke about your wife or daughters like that?" I asked, inquisitively.

Sniffing and picking something out of his teeth, he said, "Well that would never happen, coz for one thing I've got sons and for another, they're both nice looking. I can tell you feel bad for her though, but don't worry about it. It's fate, she might have done a good job, but it would have put me off my Weetabix every day having to look at that face across the office and she'd have frightened the horses, never mind the fuckin' drivers."

My only consolation was the knowledge that as long as there were Paul Tetleys in the world, there would always be a need for HR.

Chapter 11

Sex!

Sex in the workplace? Surely not?

Well, when it came to many a Harfield employee, it was a pure, unadulterated 'Yes please!' I'm still of the opinion that it shouldn't be something that should take up a lot of an HR department's time. However, I not only learned to navigate it, but I became a real expert in the secret, not so secret and downright blatantly obvious encounters that happened between many a Harfield worker. The spectrum between flirting and fornication was broad, but the time to get from one end to the other was often short.

It didn't take me much time to realise that people are not very discerning when it comes to choosing a suitable location for a quickie or a more lingering tryst. Toilet cubicles were a favourite. Even though these simple booths were often frequented, Portacabins received just as much attention. However, the disabled toilet was the trump card when it came to illicit encounters. I'm presuming that a combination of room for manoeuvre and plenty of well-secured bars upon which to lean and balance enabled maximum momentum, helping to make such a salubrious location the 'piece de resistance'.

Without a doubt, some of the Harfield workers

were enjoying a little extracurricular activity while on their shifts. The number of condoms, Femidoms, open jars of lube and discarded Mini Milk wrappers that were found in places they would never usually be, left very little to the imagination. We knew it was going on and were in general agreement that it was not ok in the workplace, but none of us had the appetite to investigate it with much gusto.

With many of the trucks distributing food, you might imagine that this would be a location to be avoided when it came to nooky, but alas, no. It turned out that Ian from Customer Services was positively electrified when it came to 'having his way' with Janine from Material Handling in the back of a truck loaded with raw protein products, no less! After they had been caught on CCTV commandeering the back of the said wagon, I had to follow this up with a meeting between Ian, Janine and warehouse manager, John.

We started with Ian, purely because he was on shift when the CCTV was being checked. Deep breath.

"Have you got a minute, Ian? John and I need to have a chat with you. Something has come to our attention. I've got some video footage here that I'd like you to watch and I need to say now that it might be uncomfortable viewing."

A bamboozled Ian, looking a bit flustered by this point, nodded and accompanied me back to my office. On playing the film, Ian turned puce with embarrassment, stuttering and stammering through an attempted explanation.

"It's not Janine's fault. It's me! She did it for me! I've got a thing for raw meat. It gets me going, big time!"

Wowsers.

Janine said the same thing along slightly more disturbing lines. It was the faint scent of animal blood that got Ian's juices following. They often got carried away when she was working on mince and he was on the shop floor to internally audit the orders. The orders weren't the only things he was auditing!

There were many more instances of workplace lust but let me dispel any myths that may be out there in terms of employer interest in their employees' sex lives. Unless you work in a particular genre of film, typically there isn't any. What people do in their own time with their bodies and with whom is quite rightly a private matter for them.

That said, sometimes and unluckily for all concerned, sex and affairs of the heart spill over into work. When people decide to 'check the oil' in the workplace or when relations start to impact a person's attendance, productivity or relationships with other colleagues, then sometimes you have to intervene. Usually, that joyous task falls at the door of the HR Department.

Allow me to re-introduce Tony Slater. Hardened warehouse manager, twenty years of distribution experience, most of which was with Harfield Distribution on the Pricetown contract. He knew how things worked. He was smart in that respect. Switched on. Operationally, nothing got past him.

He had particular idiosyncrasies, like all of us. One of which, as you've already heard, was dying his hair various shades of everything. Others included a nervous twitch which manifested itself in an involuntary neck and lower jaw movement, like a yawning giraffe with a slight shake of the head. Tony was obsessively clean-shaven, always smelled of 'Brut' and in his own eyes was never, ever wrong - a most annoying trait in my view.

Whilst Paul Tetley was outwardly foul, his words were always underpinned with humour and a glint in his eye. This let you know he was only joking and purposely trying to be outrageous. Paul never made any kind of move, proposition or used his position to manipulate people. He just said things as he saw them, with great aplomb.

Tony, on the other hand, lacked the gravitas, charm and wit to get away with some of his questionable actions or disparaging attitudes towards those who reported to him. Something just wasn't quite right, but he never did anything wrong enough to be taken to task about it. I had this ever-present, nagging feeling that one day something would come to light that would be a big deal and take some unravelling. I thought that might come in the shape of a formal complaint from one of Tony's employees. We were used to the odd minor complaint about him being unreasonable or winding people up when he had no cause. Still, there had never been any serious grievances and never anything of an overtly sexual nature. Until 'Locker Gate' that is.

One of the tasks that warehouse managers had to carry out with regular cadence was locker searches. Every shift had to undergo the examination together, leaving the shop floor with their manager to open up their compartments. It was part of the contractual agreement with Pricetown that Harfield would carry out random searches of lockers, car boots and people, the latter of which was spontaneous and unexpected, whereas locker searches took place weekly. Everyone knew that locker searches would happen; it was just a matter of when. On any given day, the shift's warehouse manager would undertake them.

Part of the search required the warehouse managers to open their lockers. This procedure was well-established and hadn't changed for years. You would therefore be forgiven for thinking that the warehouse manager in charge of shift locker searches would know well in advance when they would happen. They would consequently have their act together when it came to looking in their *own* locker.

Imagine our astonishment at Tony, when upon opening his own locker and in front of his whole shift, out fell a pair of lace knickers and dozens of polaroid pictures of Tony having his end away with Pamela Ainscough in Admin Ops! This activity was mostly on his desk, at work. Well, I say on it, it was also under it, over it and sometimes in positions I'd only ever seen in Olympic gymnastics routines until this point. This same desk was the one he shared with his colleague John and in the office where the internal window looked down on to the mezzanine area and shop floor. This work area was used to process paperwork, hold meetings and analyse management information. It clearly had an alternative and arguably much more exciting purpose - hosting all manner of sexual positions. It was an education to behold, really. Cosmopolitan would have had enough 'positions of the fortnight' to last a good few years. From my point of view, some things once seen were impossible to unsee.

It turns out that there weren't just a few photos of Tony and Pamela's illicit activity in his locker. There were a few hundred. Similar 'activities' had been going on for some time because Tony had a different hair colour in most of them and he changed it every four weeks or so on average. Jason, the union rep, who had been on shift during the search, couldn't wait to tell me what he'd found. He burst through my door, breathless with excitement and bright red, bursting to tell me what had fallen in front of him. Of all the people to accompany Tony on that particular search was the union rep, who loathed him. Jason had managed to grab the knickers and a handful of photos, run up the stairs with some gusto and promptly dump them on my desk demanding that I investigate it, in full. He spat his words out with venom and excitement, knowing that his old nemesis couldn't wriggle out of this one.

Unfortunately for Jason, it wasn't up to him to decide what happened next. I quickly informed Tom, whose most significant problem of the day up to now had been a missing pallet of hosiery on its way to Dumfries. Tom was apoplectic. Then morose. Then apoplectic again. He couldn't believe it on any level until he saw the evidence. He knew the ramifications as well as I did and that we would have to act swiftly for Tony and Pamela's sake and all concerned. Tony and Pamela were quickly suspended from work. It fell on Tom and me to look through the evidence, knickers and all and form the basis of an official investigation. Tom was disturbed by the content, on many levels.

"Bloody hell! What's he playing at? Well, hide the bloody sausage, obviously, but here at work?! They're both happily married too, allegedly. God knows how much bacteria is on that desk. I hope he didn't handle any product after a bit of 'how's your father' without washing his hands. And another thing, when did they get any bloody work done?! Can't believe we've been paying top dollar to allow a man on nights to get his end away with someone at work. I bet we're paying her double bubble 'n' all!! What a mess!! Bloody hell!"

Tom was in bits. He had worked with Tony for years, taking him under his wing; even though he found him frustrating to work with, Tom would always have Tony's back and would help him get out of whatever sticky situation in which Tony found himself. It was hard for him to find the right words, so it was mostly up to me to lead the investigation and restore some calm to the situation. Luckily, I had Jan at the end of the phone to guide me through and answer any questions as they came up. She was rightly keeping herself free for any subsequent appeal process that might arise.

Emotions were running high with everyone who worked with Tony and Pamela. Although they weren't in the workplace whilst suspended, the implications of their liaison were clear for all who had seen the unfortunate collection of stills pour out of Tony's locker. Word had soon spread across the business. Unfortunately, word had also spread outside of the warehouse, both Pamela and Tony had had to tell their other halves and children about their liaison before they heard on the local grapevine. It was gut-wrenching for them both.

In work, managers and colleagues were incredulous as the hot gossip filtered through:

'So, I suppose they'll both lose their jobs? If it were a shop floor colleague or one of my members, they would be gone for sure, straight down the road. I'm sure you'll agree as an HR professional, we can't have any double standards.' (Alex the Union representative.)

'Dirty so and so's! Will this have any impact on the numbers at all? It's imperative that we hit the budget and not be distracted by this. I suppose it might explain that missing box of condoms that we still haven't found.' (Lindsey in Accounts.)

'Did Tony's hair dye run when he was all hot and bothered in those photos? If you flick through them all quick it looks like the opening credits of 'Rainbow', only Pamela is in the frame rather than Bungle. I didn't know Tony had it in him, to be honest!' (Liz, sympathetic colleague extraordinaire.)

'How the fuck did that ugly bastard pull Pamela Ainscough? I mean, she's had more pricks in her than a dartboard, but she's fit as fuck! What is she doin' knockin' about with Wigan's answer to Michael J Fox, post - Parkinson's diagnosis! She's got no taste' (I'll give you three guesses.)

I urged my esteemed colleagues to reserve further comment and judgement until the investigation was complete and outcomes were known. They shouldn't have even seen the incriminating evidence, but I think Tom used each visit to his office as a counselling session for himself and was showing anyone who'd listen.

So, after a couple of days away from the workplace, we made enquiries about 'who knew what' regarding 'Knicker Gate'. However, nobody was admitting to knowing anything about it. Tom and I started the investigation with Pamela; we wanted her side of the story to eliminate the possibility of abuse of power at work (Tony was a couple of levels above her in the hierarchy). I tried to choose my words with care when asking her questions, but such thoughts did not trouble Pamela, who was loud and proud about her activities.

"So, tell us, love, how did it come about with Tony?" asked Tom.

"Well Tom," said Pamela flirtatiously, "it came from behind, from above, from below and sometimes from upside down, if you catch my drift?"

Her drift was not all Tom would be catching if she sat any closer to him, I silently thought.

"Are these knickers yours?" asked Tom, tentatively holding Appendix A, which was thankfully in a clear plastic bag at this stage.

"Erm… let's have a look," said Pamela, opening them up in their full glory before giving them a sniff and declaring that they were.

Not quite being able to hide his disdain, Tom continued with a contorted look on his face, "I just didn't think this was your style love."

"Well, I like doggie style, freestyle, over a stile…" Pamela offered.

"Alright, alright I don't need a blow by blow account," Tom commented, unwisely in my view.

"I'm good at that too!" Pamela cackled, playfully slapping Tom on the knee as she guffawed at her own joke. Time to get involved.

"So, Pamela, how long had you and Tony been

seeing each other?" I interjected, to prevent this from sliding further into a Benny Hill sketch.

"I don't think that's any of your business," she said, rather haughtily, probably having not noticed until this point that another female was present and the penny not quite dropping that she was subject to a formal investigation that could result in dismissal.

"Well, unfortunately, it is. I don't wish to pry; what you get up to in your own time in private is your business, but this wasn't in your own time and I think we've established that it wasn't in private either. You do understand that having sex at work with a colleague in an office shared by others is not what we pay you to do?" I asked, hopefully.

"No, but… it was only a bit of fun," she replied sheepishly. I think she was starting to realise that this wasn't just a laugh.

"Well, it isn't just that, unfortunately. I'm pretty sure it wasn't too much fun having to tell your families what's been happening or knowing that everyone you work with is now aware. You and Tony have crossed a line and we need to understand how long it's been going on for, how often it happened at work or in works time and whether or not it was consensual on both sides," I said, hoping to God that it was.

"Give over!" said Pamela incredulously. "I'm not sure what you're trying to get at, but it was just a shag. I wanted him. He wanted me. If you can't understand that sometimes it's hard to resist, even when your head is saying one thing and your fanny is saying another, then I think you need to get out more. It might help you loosen up love," she said, rolling her eyes.

"I'm alright for now, thanks. Listen, this is serious in terms of your ongoing employment with us and I need you to be open and honest with your answers. We have to conduct a full investigation and need your cooperation to do that properly. So, please could you start by telling us how and when it all began?" I thought that was the difficult spiel done. I awaited her response with bated breath.

Grimacing, Pamela reluctantly capitulated and started talking. "We've been at it for years on and off. We were at school together. I gave him a hand job at the fifth-year disco and we've been friends ever since, but I hadn't seen him for years until I started here."

Now we were getting somewhere.

"And who made the first move?" I asked, reluctantly.

"Well, our eyes just met over the shiitake mushrooms and I think we both knew we had to have each other there and then," she offered.

"Bloody hell!" murmured Tom.

"So, why did you feel the need to do this at work? Why not in private or at least off-site?" I asked, tentatively.

"Well, at first it was down to uncontrollable passion. We just couldn't help ourselves. Then it became a bit of a thrill, always wondering if we would be seen or get caught. And then, when Tony offered to film it and take pictures, I didn't know what to do with myself! My lady garden was going like the clappers, to be honest! It has a mind of its own!" She guffawed at herself. Again.

"Jesus, Mary and Joseph!" whimpered Tom whilst mopping his brow with a hanky, which was embroidered with his initials (you remember the ones).

"Well, obviously you know that it's not appropriate for that sort of thing to be happening at work?" I asked, hopefully.

"Don't tell me you've never been caught in the moment and had to surrender to your carnal callings? You're a young lass and you know how a woman has needs!" she said, utterly convinced that her behaviour was normal.

"Yes, but never at work," I replied, starting to wonder if I was the odd one.

Tom seemed to have pulled himself together a bit. "You could have been caught by anyone. What if there was an unannounced audit or customer visit when you were doing whatever it was you were doing in Tony's office? What if employees had walked in on your 'episodes'? Or, perhaps, someone was using the cherry picker and casually glanced over to the office and saw more than they bargained for? And what did you think I was paying you to do whilst you were carrying on like Syd James and

Barbara Windsor? Not to mention your marriages - both over I take it?"

"Well, yeah, but to be honest, my other half's a useless bastard anyway. Only stayed with him out of guilt coz he paid for my new tits five years back. And my new teeth. And my new kitchenette." She mused. He sounded awful. Clearly tight-fisted. "And as for getting caught, we were careful. Until our very own David Bailey fucked it right up that is. No one suspected anything and we were both up for it. Don't worry about us skiving work, Tom. Most times, it didn't last as long as the tea break and we always worked through or worked over to make sure orders went out on time. It was all just a bit of harmless fun. I fancied him. He fancied me. We had fun. We got carried away. That's all." Pamela offered, but calmly now and in a more measured way... although this was to be short-lived.

Pausing briefly for breath, she looked Tom up and down and asked in her best seductive or rather opposite of seductive voice, "Are you happily married, Tom? I give the best massages, you know; I have quite the reputation around these parts. I'm an excellent listener if ever you want to talk or look at other ways to relax. A man in your position must get very stressed. I could help with that."

"Holy Mary Mother of God... yes I am, thank you!" Tom spluttered. "I think that will do for today." He stood up, bolted for the door and left me to wrap up.

I explained to Pamela that we needed to speak with Tony next and that I would be in touch as soon as possible.

Said meeting with Tony took place later that day. At first, he seemed defensive. He was almost affronted that he'd been found out. It seemed like a real inconvenience that we were even speaking with him.

"Tell us how long this has been going on?" Tom asked.

"That's nobody's bloody business," replied, Tony indignantly. He was already twitching rapidly.

Tom lost it, clearly not in the mood for any BS or shenanigans. "Well, it is my bloody business when you're shagging a work colleague in your office who happens to be one of my employees! I'm paying you to run a shift, not a bloody knockin' shop! So do not give me any crap Tony - your job is on the line here, so I suggest you stop being a bolshy bastard and start talking!"

That got Tony's attention as he wasn't used to seeing Tom's angry side.

"Well, if you must know, it's been going on a while. We've known each other for years, but I suppose we've only been seeing each other at work for a few months. We couldn't help ourselves, but I know it went too far, to be doing that at work," Tony offered.

"You can say that again!" said Tom. "And whose are these knickers that fell out of your locker?"

"The union must have planted them there," said Tony, with no hint of irony or remorse.

"TONY!" bellowed Tom. "I've had enough bullshit to last a lifetime. Tell me the bloody truth, man!"

Tony shuffled uncomfortably in his chair, clearly not wishing to divulge any more information. Tom meanwhile was starting to look like he might have a heart attack, his brow sweating profusely, so I gently stepped in.

"The thing is, Tony, no one wants to pry, but this is about work, your credibility and trust…"

I didn't get very far before Tony snorted and looked at me like I was something he'd stepped in. I continued, unperturbed.

"The facts are that a piece of lingerie and numerous illicit photographs of you and - for want of a better phrase - a more junior employee have tumbled out of your locker. They clearly show you having sex with her, on your desk, in your office, presumably in work time as you will have been the only manager on shift. Not only is this completely unacceptable in itself, but there are questions around you using your senior position at work to have sex with a more junior employee, whether it was consensual or not. Your credibility is shot, your job is on the line and you seem to be suggesting that the union representatives we have on-site planted a pair of knickers in your locker. We can get them in and you can look them in the eye and ask them if you like, but the best chance of you salvaging anything from this situation is, to tell the truth about what happened."

Tony shifted uncomfortably in his chair.

"Right, well they are Pamela's knickers, obviously, but I don't remember putting them there. They must have been left behind after one of our meetings. I suppose I just buried them in there, thinking it was a better option than the office bin. As for the photos, we both agreed it would be fun to do and everything we ever did was consensual - I'm not a monster. Things are not great at home and my daughter is having a few problems, which means my wife is too knackered to do anything in bed, so I've looked elsewhere. I'm sorry for doing this at work, Tom and if it puts you in an awkward position at all, it will end here and I swear I won't do anything like this again. Please don't sack me - my marriage is all but over, but I still need to feed my kids. I'll do anything - I'll have counselling - anything."

"Mmm," pondered Tom. "One more thing. What were you thinking organising a locker search when you knew that those photos and things were in your locker and there was a strong chance that people might find them?" Tony just stared at Tom. He didn't say anything. He didn't have to. I knew in that instant, in that heartbeat moment that Tony had wanted to get caught.

Briefly pulling himself together, Tony just said

"I wasn't thinking straight," which Tom seemed to buy for now.

We adjourned the meeting. Considering everything, really and truly Tony should have lost his job - he'd committed several sackable offences. But Tom was torn, having worked with him for years. I offered my theory that Tony had wanted us to find out. However, this couldn't be proven and I wasn't convinced that Tom wanted to believe that.

In the end, Tom put his neck on the line for Tony. He tore strips off him behind closed doors, but to the people he was accountable to - his boss, the customer, the employees - he refused to give further details of the situation. Tom only said that there were many sides to a story and, given Tony's previous good record, his commitment to getting counselling and that this would never happen again, Tony would remain a member of the management team and keep his job. Though he did receive a final written warning. Jan and I had insisted on it with Tom - there had to be some sort of sanction for this. Pamela received the same disciplinary outcome and was moved to another department with another manager (another man though, which she fully embraced as a new opportunity!)

Neither of them appealed against the formal outcome. Anyone would have been forgiven for thinking that was the end of the matter. Any normal person would have kept their head down, got on with their job and been humbled by the whole experience. Tony continued to dye his hair, take exception if anyone ever had a different opinion to him on anything and demand that people were sacked if they even looked at him wrongly. It wasn't the type of culture where you removed people, so we all just accepted that this was Tony. Life went on, for the time being anyway.

It was time to get organised for the 'Christmas Do' again. Blimey.

Chapter 12

LITTLE JIMMY URINE AND THE CHRISTMAS FESTIVITIES

Having seen the kinds of things that can happen at Christmas parties for a few years now, I thought a change was in order. I embarked on a mission to upgrade the Christmas do from working men's clubs to something more salubrious. In my naivety, I thought that if we showed some respect to and investment in the employees, they would return the favour by behaving properly at the party. There were some doubters.

"Bullshit!" said Tony Slater. "You could put this shower of shite in the Ritz and they'd turn it into a chimps' tea party."

"We've been going to the Working Men's Club for years," Tom pointed out. "It might be a bit tired, but anything too posh and we might not be able to do the meat raffle. Folk put their glad rags on just for the chance of winning a month's worth of red meat and offal. I'm not sure we can change that now love, there'll be an uproar!"

"And how much will all that cost?" asked Lindsey, pursed lips and all. Luckily, I was well prepared. Jan was on-side, as were my payroll team, who would help organise the event and distribute tickets. The Sports and Social Committee (run by employees for employees) which everyone paid into each year, also fancied a change. They agreed to match fund any uplift in costs that may occur. I had run it by the union and they were supportive of a new approach. We all thought everyone would enjoy a coach trip with their families to see the panto one weekend. For the main Christmas party, we proposed going to a Manchester hotel with the option of staying over if we could secure a discounted room rate. Tom could see that I'd done my homework. He got key personnel on board and eventually agreed that we could give it a go. This deal was on the strict understanding that if anything went 'tits up' or we couldn't hold the meat raffle, we'd revert to the club again the following year, no questions asked.

We had an agreement.

Before too long, we'd ascertained that there was plenty of interest in the panto. I booked coaches from Warrington, St Helens and Wigan to carry employees and their families to see 'Snow White and the Seven Dwarves' in Manchester. It boasted an all-star cast with actors from 'Hi-de-hi', 'Allo 'Allo and several people who had made regular appearances on 'Blankety Blank'. All in all, it passed off without major incident, apart from uncorroborated reports of Tony Slater heckling obscenities at Snow White throughout the performance and the odd sneaking of cans into the show. I think the latter would have gone mostly unnoticed if one of the warehouse operatives hadn't done a wee into his empty tin of

Skol, placed it on the floor, then knocked it over, spilling it everywhere - on people's coats, their handbags and ridiculously expensive pick n mix. His excuse? 'I was slap bang in the middle of row M, love - it would have disrupted the performance and pissed off a lot more people if I'd tried to shuffle my arse to the gents halfway through Act Two!' He had a point, but still.

All in all, the panto was a great success and (following the dry cleaning) we agreed we'd do it again the following year. The upgraded Christmas party, a couple of weeks later may have needed a little more persuasion.

In the planning stages, I took a couple of employees from the Sports and Social Committee with me to meet Tracey at the Britannia Hotel in Manchester. She could not have been more helpful. Having secured a discounted room rate of £45, including breakfast (a bargain for December) and receiving confirmation, in blood, that the meat raffle would be permitted, I left the committee members to organise the party in the way they knew best.

We promoted the event and tickets flew out of the payroll office. People seemed keen at the prospect of dressing up for a city centre bash and they welcomed the change of venue. The big night came along and we were ready and up for it. Spouses, partners and significant others were invited on this occasion. Matt was looking forward to it, so I booked us into the hotel for the evening. I knew I would be taking it steady as there would inevitably be something to 'deal with' and it was always best to be sober for it.

A few of the managers had also decided to stay over. Matt did me proud socialising with everyone and it was nice to meet some of my colleague's partners and see a different side to them. Tom's wife was the boss at home, but nice enough. Jan's husband was friendly and I was made up for my old mucker, Dawn, who brought her new boyfriend to meet us all for the first time. He was great and worked at a Harfield site in South Yorkshire. He knew some of the team already and there was plenty of relatable banter. Surprisingly, Tony Slater's wife came along. She was lovely - super shy and quiet, but charming and she made an effort to get to know everyone. I felt sorry for her being married to the twitching lothario of the north west, but they seemed to be trying to work things out. It didn't stop him from flirting with anything in a party hat though, albeit that most people shifted away from him at quite a pace as soon as he approached.

Liz's latest squeeze was very amusing - big personality, big drinker and big hairy chest exposed for everyone to see and later fondle on the dancefloor. John's wife, Joan, was very pleasant and as dedicated as John to doing things right. I could tell this from the way they both counted 'one-two-three-four' loudly as they danced/marched across the dancefloor for most of the evening.

Then there was Paul and his wife Dot. We had a

drink with them at the hotel bar as we were checking in. They had been married forever, had twin sons in their early twenties and a young grandson who was the apple of their eye. They were like Jack and Vera Duckworth from Coronation Street - they bickered a lot and Dot gave Paul the occasional slap as they were talking, but only when he said something completely outlandish (which was quite often). Anyone could see that they loved each other and this shone through. I was pleased that Matt had got a chance to meet Paul. Matt had heard plenty of stories and now he could finally meet the dichotomy - this genius logistics guru and legal liability rolled into one. He was hilarious though and Matt could see this. They got on well as Paul gave him advice on everything from football to the success of a happy marriage.

A short while later, as we went up to the room to get ready, we realised that we were on the same floor. The rooms were awful - cramped, pokey and no en-suite bathroom. Good job we'd showered before we left, I guess, but could I complain for £45? Probably not.

Paul suggested that we knocked on the door for him when we were ready and we could go to the main event together. Innocent enough, I thought. It made sense - safety in numbers and all that. So, about an hour later, with our glad rags firmly on, Matt and I strolled down the corridor and tentatively knocked on Paul and Dot's door. There was no answer initially. Whilst we were waiting, I noticed that the door opposite their room was slightly ajar - or off the latch as we'd say. Hearing a bit of commotion, I pushed the door open to see Shaun Richardson, from the shop floor proudly pissing into the kettle whilst whistling a tune from South Pacific. I think I let out a little yelp as he turned to see me saying "What the fuck…?"

"Sorry, sorry - I didn't mean to," I started to fluster with Matt giggling behind me before adding, "actually, what are you doing Shaun? Where's Louise?" Louise being Shaun's wife, whom I'd met a couple of times previously.

"She's gone to use the bathroom down the hall, which, by the way, is always fucking full, so I thought I'd take a quick one in here and empty it later. My options were limited, love," he said, as Paul joined us in the corridor.

"Well, maybe next time, you should lock the door? Or maybe walk down the one flight of stairs to the bar and use the Gents there?" I countered.

Looking at Matt, he said, "Mate, don't tell me you've never pissed in a wardrobe or a kettle when needs must?" he implored.

Matt didn't deny it straight away. I was starting to reconsider my life choices fleetingly whilst simultaneously making a mental note to carry a travel kettle with me from this point onwards, when Tony Slater appeared in the hallway.

"Now then. You lot alreet? Tony asked, adjusting

his tie and twitching as per the norm. Barely being able to take my eye off his ruby fusion hair colour, (which I could have sworn was more of a sunflower blonde the previous day) I said we were fine and did not mention recent events.

"Is Suzanne not with you?" I asked him.

"No, she's having a lie-down, a bit of a rest before dinner. She'll need it after what we've been doing, nudge-nudge, wink-wink! I'm just off to see what other 'tottie' there might be downstairs. Never too early to bang some new beaver!" he said, with no sense of disloyalty to his lovely wife at all.

I gave Paul a knowing look, begging him to read my mind.

"No rush, Tony," he said. "Matt and Gemma were just going to join me for a cup of coffee, maybe with a drop of whiskey if you'd care to join us? Kettle's just on in Shaun's room."

"Well, that's very civilised of you, Paul," said Tony, clearly pleased as punch that any of his work colleagues' would want to spend any more time with him, "don't mind if I do."

"Excellent." I said, "you boys have that first cup and I'll go and grab some more mugs from our room," before turning to Matt and whispering to him not to drink any. I think my advice was superfluous to requirements though with Matt having seen what was in the kettle.

The rest of the evening unfolded pretty much as expected; most people were having fun and behaving themselves and others not so much. As soon as I'd made my way downstairs, Tracey made me aware of an incident. It wasn't even 7 o'clock. The first rumpus had happened on one of the buses en-route to the venue. A fight had broken out. A group of lads had been drinking all afternoon ahead of the party. One of them thought another had been chatting up his missus. Punches were thrown and fisticuffs took place. They arrived at the door covered in blood but were allowed in by one of the beefy bouncers on the understanding that they got cleaned up, pronto. He didn't hear a peep out of them for the rest of the evening. Two short hours later, they were dancing on each other's shoulders to 'Hi Ho Silver Lining' in a playful way and all was good with the world.

Next, I was made aware of a kerfuffle in the disabled toilet. Paul Tetley had uncovered a cocaine party involving half a dozen employees who had been snorting it off the toilet seat. They were absolutely off their heads and had to leave. Most of the gang worked in the warehouse, but one of them was a driver for Paul. I arrived on the scene as Paul had him pinned against a wall ready to throttle him. I pulled Paul off him and said we'd take it up properly on Monday, back in work. He relented and let the lad go, but not before wagging a disappointed finger at him and shouting that he 'wasn't having fuckin' Zammo driving any of his trucks, End of!'

Then, some party games got a bit out of hand as people took their turn at Space Hopper races. They were taking it a little too seriously and ended up smashing through some tables close to the dance floor. Arguably, this was our fault for organising them in the first place. There was a temporary halt to proceedings as I helped clean up the smashed glasses whilst apologising profusely.

You would think that that would be enough for one evening. Surely, I wouldn't have to worry about any managers or directors of the business. To be fair, I didn't until the following morning when certain things came to light.

Take George Pickwick, a big wig in the Harfield family. He was an Area Director who was based at Harfield HQ. George looked after multiple contracts in addition to our own; he was Tom's boss. His key responsibilities involved overseeing performance across the group and sharing best practice across numerous sites. However, on this particular stormy December evening, he was far from focused on his area director duties. Instead, he was channelling all of his energy into Jackie Summerbee, a purchasing director who also worked at group level for Harfield.

George and Jackie had been seated together at the 'Aspirations' Conference that had taken place earlier in the year at the Royal Hotel in Manchester city centre. They had met a few times before but did not know each other well. It's safe to say that their (highly intimate, as it was to turn out) knowledge of each other increased as the evening progressed.

George and Jackie had, by all accounts, been

hitting the free bar hard. Flash forward four hours and the pair had now hit the bedroom with equal dedication. The trouble was that they had both consumed enough Tia Maria to sink a ship and their faculties were decidedly impaired. This didn't stop a steamy night of passion, far from it! A very sexually satisfied, yet butt naked, George had stumbled to the toilet door, opened it with force, staggered inside and pulled the door shut behind him. Only this door wasn't the door to the toilet; it was the door out of the hotel room. And now George was wandering down the corridor in his birthday suit, making a beeline for the giant pot that contained a rather flaccid looking cheese plant.

It was at the point where George was in the throes of treating the plant to a plentiful golden shower that the night porter turned into this very corridor to be greeted with two very pale, tired-looking buttocks. Unfortunately, George had no recollection of either his own room number or Jackie Summerbee's. He had to accompany said night porter to reception to find out where his bed was for the night. Luckily for George, the chap was either a very decent sort or simply didn't wish to feast his eyes on George's manhood for any longer than necessary. He opened a housekeeping cupboard on the way to reception and produced a large towel for George to wrap himself in whilst they found his room number.

You would think George would have been satisfied with this show of kindness; instead, he went on to demand to be told Jackie Summerbee's room number from the poor receptionist. George was a man full of self-importance and was not used to people refusing him what he wanted. Eventually, accepting that the receptionist would not divulge this information, he scuttled back to his own room, with his well-worked tail quite literally hanging between his legs.

Being the HR person on duty, I was charged with having to investigate all the events of that evening. The hotel, the coach company and Zammo all made official complaints. It was not easy trying to unpick the finer details. George was mortified and in fear of losing his job. Rumours were spreading about his liaison with Jackie and his naked trip to the front lobby. Unable to comprehend his 'fucking stupidity', he simply repeated the line, 'bloody Chocolate Torte! Why didn't I stop things there and just leave it at that?!'

In true 'jobs for the boys' style, it was left to Ian Park, Group Head of HR for the whole of Harfield Distribution to speak to George about his misdemeanours; how he'd brought the company into disrepute, setting a terrible example to employees. There are often different rules for those at the top. I don't think it's right or how it should work, but it is a reality. I think, in practice, this consisted of Ian and George sharing a bottle of single malt, slapping each other on the back and having a right laugh about what had happened. Hilarious. Nothing was ever said to Jackie, as far as I'm aware.

As for the other cases, 'drugs gate' proved interesting. Two of the employees present admitted to it but tried to argue that they weren't at work, so it didn't count. Two others argued most vehemently that they were not taking drugs. They were simply in the same room, despite their noses looking like they'd been dipped in flour when we arrived. Paul Tetley's driver was caught red-handed and admitted to his crimes, resigning before Paul could get his hands on him again. The driver did object to being called 'Zammo' when it had been supposedly a one-off high for him. But when Paul threatened to shove his drugs where the sun doesn't shine, he backed off. I think the driver was scared that Paul would follow his threat through. All of this took place well before the introduction of 'substance misuse' policies. We were navigating our way through it all as we went along. The group were all dismissed on the grounds of gross misconduct and for bringing the company into disrepute. All accepted their fate and nobody appealed.

In terms of Harfield's answer to Mike Tyson and Ricky Hatton, they were both issued with final written warnings. They did appeal, arguing that they were not at work when the fighting happened. They claimed that it was over 'sommat and nowt' and they were 'happy as Larry' a couple of hours later. We did have to apologise to the coach company, the other employees on the bus and their spouses.

Really and truly it sounded more like a slapstick comedy than a case of common assault. The two lads had no qualms about working together.

The truth was that this sort of thing happened a lot - more often than anyone cares to think about in the cold light of day when at work. Even the hotel told us that it was a widespread activity, if a little unsavoury. Our approach was to say that, whilst we accept that people were not 'at work' as such, they were still representing the company and their behaviour should reflect this; a typical approach and one that has been taken in every business I've worked in. The key lies in making sure the workforce is made aware of this too - basically, they are ambassadors for the company when attending functions. Employees should act like they are at work in terms of their actions and behaviours. On the other hand, employers should extend their duty of care when organising functions - it's as simple as that. I was on a mission to make this clear on every event poster, ticket and even in the employee handbook going forward, so there was never any room for doubt.

On the brighter side of things, at least Tom's wife won the meat raffle, which for her was tantamount to winning the lottery - happy days!

A couple of months after this event, when things at work had returned to normal, my thoughts turned to organising a summer barbecue. I was at home with Matt one Monday morning, having booked a long weekend off work. The phone rang and it was Linda, Tom's PA, in a terrible fluster.

"I'm so sorry to bother you love, but I don't know what else to do!" she said in a shaky voice.

"What is it?" I asked, "Whatever it is, just take your time and I'll help."

"It's this video on the shared drive. I've just come into work, tapped on my keyboard and it was already logged in. It's unusual as I always take good care to close everything down properly before the weekend. There's a video, well several actually, of Tony Slater. You can tell it's him because he's twitching and he's erm well he's pleasuring himself in one video and in another he's just bent over, parting his arse cheeks at the camera. I feel sick. It's put me right off my breakfast peach. It's not what anyone wants to see first thing in the morning."

So, after a quick chat with Tom, who was mostly monosyllabic and mortified by the discovery, in I went, holiday cancelled. Liz and I investigated the footage and spoke with Tony and Linda. We concluded pretty quickly that we would invite Tony to a formal disciplinary meeting. The footage was pretty much as Linda had described, but Liz and I had to sit through three or four different films of Tony doing things to himself that could only have been for his own pleasure. It wasn't pretty. He'd strategically positioned a camera to film all of this and himself in front of it.

"Well, this is a bloody education, isn't it love?"

said Liz as we crooked our necks to see precisely what Tony was trying to show us. Posting it on the shared drive at work could only mean one thing - he definitely wanted it to be seen. We quickly removed it from the public space to save other people's blushes as it was already playing on a loop in reception, but some of the staff had seen it by the time we spoke with Tony.

"It was an accident," he said when we presented him with his work. Liz and I simply made a note of Tony's responses, but the same answers wouldn't wash with Tom when it came to the disciplinary meeting. Banging the investigation report onto the table with a thud that meant business, Tom was giving Tony short shrift this time.

"Another 'accident' Tony? Bollocks man. Would you know what the truth looked like if it bit you on your scraggy white arse?" enquired Tom. Good. I could leave Tom to lead the conversation whilst he was in no mood for Tony's nonsense.

"I didn't mean to do it. I mean, I meant to film myself, but it was meant for my satisfaction. I thought I was sending it to my personal email address, but obviously, I didn't," Tony offered.

"You would have had to go out of your way to sit at Linda's desk, log on to her computer, open the shared drive whilst on a weekend shift when very few of the office staff were in and upload videos from wherever it was you had them," I surmised.

"I just wanted to find a peaceful corner on Saturday

after most people had left. I was interrupted by the cleaners, which is why I didn't log off. I genuinely had no idea that I had uploaded that content onto the shared drive. I mean, why would I do that?" The look on his face feigned innocence whilst all the time, it was undeniable that he wanted it to be seen. He didn't care who he took with him on his voyeurism ride.

There was no getting out of this one. Tom's patience had finally run out. He didn't go mad; he didn't lose his temper; he just asked me the best way to get rid of Tony as we adjourned the meeting. We decided that dismissal on the grounds of gross misconduct and breakdown of trust and confidence in the working relationship was best. Tony was invited to a meeting to receive his fate and didn't take it well. He appealed against the decision, but there were no tender mercies shown by Jan and Tom's boss, George Pickwick. They politely explained to Tony that he was lucky that the police hadn't been involved on the grounds of indecent exposure.

"You should have got rid of the dirty perv after that last incident, Tom!" bellowed George.

"I know, but we all make 'mistakes' don't we George?" said Tom cuttingly. "I just wanted to give the guy a second chance, which he has literally spuffed in my face!" said Tom, all forlorn.

As I said earlier, word had got around and people had seen the footage. It was just as Tony had wanted, I suspect.

"Well, I wouldn't be braggin' about that and showing it to all and sundry! It's a right chode!" Said Liz, who was disappointed at what she'd had to look at during the investigation.

"Disgusting. Tony needs horsewhipping," said Lindsey with great charm. She was on the same wavelength as Jason, the union rep, who thought flagellation and a dose of the rack would help teach Tony the lesson he deserved. Disturbing, to say the least.

"I shared an office and a desk with Tony and others, it would seem, for many years. I did not know that this was something he did. Although it might account for those random sticky stains on the floor. I just thought someone had dropped a cheesecake," said John innocently.

"He might well have a chipolata, but hats off to him - he played the hand that life dealt him very well," offered Paul Tetley. "Still don't know how he pulled Pamela Ainscough, mind you."

"Enough!" said Tom. "I am scarred by what I have seen. For those of you who were lucky enough not to see the footage, count your bloody blessings and move on. For those who did see it, we will pay for full counselling for as long as any of you need it. Now. Let's crack on with business. What's first on the agenda?"

"This year's Summer Do!" said Liz.

Blimey.

Epilogue

So, now the first part of the ride on our HR girl's equivalent of the Wild Mouse at Blackpool has come to an end. You might perhaps feel incredulous at some of the tales that you have been told, but this was a different time and place, a different era altogether, rooted in the north of England. It was another world, a world that is difficult to comprehend today.

But these sorts of things did happen - day in, day out.

This particular ride helped me to understand what makes people tick more than anything else could. The uncensored world that I lived and breathed in provided a baptism of fire of the highest degree. That said, the warm beating heart of this dysfunctional Harfield family was never to be underestimated.

Those first few years at Harfield Distribution were undoubtedly some of the happiest of my career. I learned so much from Jan, Dawn and the people I was surrounded by. At times I had to think on my feet, but always felt grateful for the big safety net around me - something you don't have to the same extent when you step into more senior management roles. Jan and Dawn became friends of mine for life and I couldn't have asked for a better start.

The team and I lived through some pretty big moments together, including the dawn of a new millennium. We breathed a collective sigh of relief as the dreaded Y2K Millennium Bug never really happened. We saw the building of the Millennium Dome and its swift demise when it closed twelve months later. Eventually, it became the O2 arena. Big Brother was launched, changing reality TV forever.

In the years to come, we watched in horror as the planes flew into the Twin Towers, thinking it was a film at first on the daytime news. We watched those Twin Towers tumble to the ground, firefighters going in one direction and the rest of New York in another. It was horrific; there were no reference points to ground people or help them make sense of it, because it was like nothing the world had ever seen before. It changed the world forever.

As a country, we went to war in Iraq shortly afterwards. The impact of this on our workforce was significant. Some of our employees lost sons and daughters in the war, whereas others had much more pressing issues to worry about - in their heads.

For example, "Is there any chance that you could lend your support to my campaign relating to the war in Iraq?" enquired Jason one day.

"Tell me more," I said, innocently, thinking he might be raising money for the families of victims of war, or sending parcels to our soldiers in the desert.

"Well, I'm petitioning Granada Tonight and the whole of ITV as it goes, because I can't be the only one who feels strongly about this," he proposed.

"Go on," I said eagerly and with bated breath, hoping for a telethon or a slot on Granada Tonight.

"Well, since this fiasco began, the TV schedules have gone to pot and I haven't been able to record re-runs of 'Prisoner Cell Block H' or 'Kojak' with any kind of consistency. It's messing with my mind and the lady wife is considering going back to beta-blockers. Whoever decided that it's ok to plaster ITN newsflashes all over regional programming and interfere with the progress of the great bald detective or the fate of the ladies in Wentworth needs tarring and feathering. It's not right!"

Amazing.

Unfortunately, I was unable to help Jason. Instead, I put my energies into making sure that our employees who had lost loved ones in the conflict were given compassionate leave and a lot of leeway, owing to the horrendous circumstances.

The early part of the new millennium was promising – at least in terms of the economy, but this was before the Iraq war and the widespread 2008 crash. The business environment was evolving and we knew things were about to change on the work front. There was talk of takeovers, mergers and, depending on who bought what, potential divestitures. One possible option was that Pricetown would bring their warehousing and distribution operations in-house. This proposition would mean uncertainty for our sites. Why pay a third party? We could all sense that change was coming, in one form or another, just from the volume of information I was being asked to provide and the regularity of it. Conjecture amongst my colleagues was taking up a lot of thinking time and was the main topic of chat amongst the management team. I decided to place it to one side as best I could and get on with the day-to-day challenges in the only way I knew. It was all speculation until we were told otherwise, so I tried not to let it take up too much headspace until we had confirmation of any actual transitions.

Change did eventually arrive and the impact was notable, resulting in new career openings for some and opportunities outside the business for others. Nothing lasts forever as they say.

For the time being, I got on with my work and focused on planning mine and Matt's big day. I was made up when my colleagues willingly gave up ten minutes of their lunch breaks, including the payroll team, in the weeks leading up to our wedding. We practised 'Reach for the Stars' by 'S Club 7' with great gusto ahead of the main event. As such, they were all able to join in with Matt, the bridesmaids, the best man and ushers as we undertook our first dance.

Even Paul Tetley threw his hands up to the tune (under threat of Dot) and told me I looked 'crackin' on the big day, which was as civil as I'd ever heard him. He even said that Matt was a 'lucky fella' in fatherly tones, in a poignant moment when it was just him and me at the bar. Mind you, he ruined it two minutes later when Matt came over and he administered a manly slap on the back, wishing him best of luck trying to 'pound the punanni pavement after a skinful'.

And there was more wisdom to impart.

"The thing is, son, you might be best getting a good night's kip now and spearing the bearded clam as the sun comes up and your dawn horn kicks in. Doggy style, obviously. No one wants morning breath, even on honeymoon." Incredible insight. Always.

Off we went on honeymoon with Paul's fatherly advice ringing in our ears. Luckily, I got to work with him and a number of my old Harfield colleagues, for a good while longer. It was undoubtedly an ongoing education.

I didn't know it at the time, but, the best and most challenging adventures in my HR career were still to come.

Although the stories I've just related were a cracking warm-up act.

'Now we know where we're going, baby,
We can lay back and enjoy the ride.'
The Seahorses – *Love is the Law* (1997)

ACKNOWLEDGEMENTS

There are so many people to thank who inspired this book and helped us to get it off the ground. We've had a ball, constructing the fictional world of Harfield Distribution and hope you have been as entertained reading the stories as we have been writing it.

We'd like to start by thanking Sunday days and Thursday evenings for being reliably available during the writing of this labour of love. Without these days of the week, usually reserved for relaxing and doing nothing, we wouldn't have found the time. Equally, without the constant supplies of hummus, peppers and vegetable crisps, we're not sure our creative juices would have flowed as freely. Yes, we really were that wild.

To our parents and closest friends who have been encouraging the idea of this book for years, saying it would make amusing or interesting reading, I hope we fulfilled the remit. Thank you for your unwavering support throughout, for taking the time to read and re-read first drafts and most of all for being honest when we needed you to be. We could not have done this without your open-mindedness, the time you took to read things through and your candid feedback. Never change.

To our husbands and children who gave us the time and space to put pen to paper, thank you for your sustenance and squeezes. It's all for you guys in the end.

To everyone E worked with, in the early years of what continues to be a most enjoyable HR career, I owe you so much. Thank you for coaching, mentoring, shaping, shocking and inspiring in all the right ways. In particular, Jane, Diane and Paul who have become lifelong friends, reminding me throughout the writing process about some of the crazy things we lived through and managed.

To Rick and the team at Fisher King Publishing who had the faith to publish a gaggle of ideas loosely rooted in the working world of HR. Thank you for taking a punt on us and helping a dream to become a reality.

To J from E, I'm so pleased we went for lunch that day to Salts Mill and you listened to me ranting about this idea I had for a book. It wouldn't have seen the light of day without your contributions and for that, I am truly grateful. Thank you for your spectacular turn of phrase, for putting your foot down when certain items were too outrageous to include and for the sparkle that you bring to the party.

Finally, thank you to all who took the time to read our jaunt. Hopefully, you had the odd belly laugh and an occasional tear. We remain blown away by your support - thank you.